The Lone Pilgrim

ALSO BY LAURIE COLWIN

Passion and Affect   (*stories*)
Shine On, Bright and Dangerous Object
Happy All the Time

THE
LONE
PILGRIM

Stories by

Laurie Colwin

PERENNIAL LIBRARY

Harper & Row, Publishers, New York
Grand Rapids, Philadelphia, St. Louis, San Francisco
London, Singapore, Sydney, Tokyo, Toronto

First PERENNIAL LIBRARY edition published 1990.

LIBRARY OF CONGRESS CATALOG CARD NUMBER 89-45642

ISBN 0-06-097270-X

90 91 92 93 94   FG   10 9 8 7 6 5 4 3 2 1

To Juris Jurjevics
Nancy and Jonathan Aldrich
and
Victoria Wilson

Contents

The Lone Pilgrim

The Lone Pilgrim

I have been the house pet to several families: friendly, cheerful, good with children, and, most important, I have an acute sensitivity to the individual rhythms of family life. I blend in perfectly, without losing myself. A good houseguest is like an entertainer: Judy Garland, Alfred Hitchcock, Noel Coward. You know what a specific public wants—in my case, groups of two, with children.

For example, Paul and Vera Martin and their children, Ben and Violet. Paul and Vera are lawyers. Paul spends rainy Sundays fishing, and although Vera is a good cook, she is not fond of cleaning fish, so Paul's grandfather's knife is entrusted to me. I do the neat job of a surgeon. Vera, who likes precision, was so impressed by my initial performance that she allowed me into her kitchen, and we have been cooking together ever since. I knew by instinct where she would keep her pots, her baking dishes, her mixing bowls, her silverware. If you are interested in people, their domestic arrangements are of interest, too. That's the sort of student of human conduct I am.

In Maine, I visit Christopher and Jean Goodison and their little son Jean Luc. The Goodisons are haphazard housekeepers, but I have their routine down pat. Their baby and I get along famously. We have a few moments together: a hailstorm he observed from my lap; a lesson in crawling; an afternoon with a kitten. The best way with babies, I have come to know, is quietude. Never approach first. Be casual. Pay minimal tactile attention, and never try to make them love you. You can sit on the same sofa with a child and do nothing more than clutch its little foot from time to time, and before long you will have that child on your lap.

The Goodisons will leave Jean Luc with me when they go shopping, although ordinarily—with ordinary mortals, that is—they are very protective of their son. When they return, I surprise them with a Lady Baltimore cake. Alone in their house, I admire their Shaker table, the fancy-back spoons I find mixed in with their spatulas, the dried-flower arrangements in their lusterware pitchers.

And there are others: the Hartwells in Boston, who live in a Spartan apartment decorated with city-planning charts. The rigorous Mazzinas, who take me camping. The Jerricks, who dress for dinner and bring you a breakfast tray on Sunday morning: coffee, toast, and a small vase with a single flower in it. My friends admire my charm, my sagacity, my propriety, and my positive talent for fitting in with the daily life of others while holding my own.

The adhesive tape on my mailbox reads "P. Rice." Paula Rice, that is, known to all as Polly. I am the charming girl illustrator. I did the pictures for *Hector the Hero, The Pig Who Said Pneu, Fish with Feathers, Snow White and Rose Red*, and *The I Don't Care Papers*—all children's books. Five feet four, reddish hair, brown eyes, long legs. At college, I studied medieval French literature, but kept a sketchbook with me at all times. During the summers, I studied calligraphy, papermaking, and bookbinding, and worked as an apprentice at the Lafayette Press, printers of fine editions. I make a living illustrating children's books, but to please myself I do etchings and ink drawings, which I often present to friends on special occasions—marriages, anniversaries, birthdays.

On the side, I am a perfect houseguest. I have the temperament for it. Being a designer teaches you the habit of neatness, and an appreciation for a sense of order not your own. Being a houseguest allows you to fantasize with no one crowding you. After all, you are but a guest, an adornment. Your object is to give pleasure to your hosts. Lolling around in other people's houses allows your mind to drift. Inspired by my surroundings, I indulge myself in this lazy, scene-setting kind of thought. For example: a big yellow moon; the kitchen of an old house in an academic community. On the window ledge a jar of homemade jam, a pot of chives, a cutting of grape ivy in a cracked mug. A big dog sleeps in front of the stove. If you open the window, you feel the crisp October air. An apple pie or a loaf of bread is in the oven, and the house is warm with the scent of it. You wonder if it is time to deal with the last pumpkin, or to pickle the basket of green tomatoes. In the study, your husband is drowsing over an elevating book, a university-press book in blue wrappers. You are wearing a corduroy skirt, a chic blouse, and a sweater of your husband's is tied around your shoulders. You are a woman contemplating seasonal change.

Or you go to the Martins on a rainy night. They occupy two floors of a Victorian brownstone, and as you contemplate the polished moldings and watch the rain through the leaded windows, you feel you are in England in the spring—in a little house in Devizes, say, or Bexhill-on-Sea. Your children have just been put to bed. You have finished reading a book on the life of Joseph Wright of Derby. There is a knock on the door. You start up. Your husband is away, and it is foggy outside. At the door is an old lover, someone who broke your heart, who is in England on business and has tracked you down.

Of course, the fact of the matter is that you live in a flat in New York. Your work is done at an oak drawing table, surrounded by pots of brushes and pens. In other people's houses your perspective widens. You contemplate the Martins' old Spode platter. You know the burn on their dining-room table —the only flaw in its walnut surface—is from Paul's cigar, placed there the night before Ben was born. These details feed the imagination.

Oh, domesticity! The wonder of dinner plates and cream pitchers. You know your friends by their ornaments. You want everything. If Mrs. A. has her mama's old jelly mold, you want one, too, and everything that goes with it—the family, the tradition, the years of having jelly molded in it. We domestic sensualists live in a state of longing, no matter how comfortable our own places are.

You cannot be a good houseguest and be married. Single, you carry only the uncluttered luggage of your own personality, selected and packed by only one pair of hands. Marriage is two-dimensional to the unmarried. No matter how close they get to a couple, they view the situation without any depth perception. If companionship is what you want, and you don't have it, any part of it looks good, including complaints, squabbles, misunderstandings. If only, you feel, you had someone close enough to misunderstand. Intimate enough to squabble with. Well known enough to complain about. Marriage is a condition, like neatness, or order. It is as safe as the wedding silver on the sideboard. To the unmarried, marriage is a sort of trapping, right down to the thin, unobtrusive gold bands.

That's romanticism for you. No one fantasizes about dreary afternoons, despair, unreasonableness, chaos, and boredom. Not the unmarried, that is—especially if they contemplate marriage from a perch of well-savored solitude. Solitude provides you the luxury of thinking about the closed, graceful shapes of other people's lives. My friends are steady, just like me. But, steady as I am, why am I so solitary? No matter how orderly, measured, and careful my arrangements are, they are only a distillation of me, not a fusion of myself and someone else. I have my domestic comforts, except that mine are only mine.

My life changed with the appearance into it of Gilbert Seigh. It was for Gilbert that I produced my best work: illustrations for *The Art of Courtly Love* and *The Poems of Marie de France*.

Gilbert's father, grandfather, and great-grandfather had been publishers of fine editions. After practicing law for five years, Gilbert took over the business when his father's eyesight began to fail. Gilbert was born into the business and was infected with it. His great-grandfather did editions of James Fenimore Cooper, Thackeray, and Mrs. Scott Courrier-Maynard, a now unknown poet of Connecticut. His grandfather went in for U.S. Grant's memoirs, Washington Irving, and speeches of American presidents. Gilbert's father did the poets of his day, edited and published a little magazine called *Lampfire*, and produced double-language volumes of Rimbaud, Rilke, and Christian Morgenstern. Gilbert goes in for the classics, for naturalist works, and for Melville. Three thousand dollars will get you the Seigh Press edition of "Billy

Budd." Six will get you his two volumes of *Wild Flowers of the North American Continent*.

Gilbert does not look like a man of books. He looks like a young auto magnate: large, ruddy, and enthusiastic. His glasses fog over from sheer enjoyment. He has a hot temper and a big, loud laugh. I often picture him in his leather chair at his office, laughing and wiping his glasses on the vest of his woolly suit. I like to watch him go up against his master binder, a fiery Italian named Antonio Nello, fighting about the ornaments for a spine. This clash of hardheaded perfectionists brings forth stubborn shouting from Gilbert and operatic flights of invective from Antonio, after which the correct solution is reached.

Several months after I met Gilbert, I fell in love with him. I was sent to him by Paul Martin. Gilbert, at dinner with Paul and Vera, had said he was looking for an illustrator and couldn't find one whose work he liked. He had been to dozens of galleries, museums, and agents. He had looked through hundreds of illustrated books. Then Paul showed him a drawing I had done to celebrate the birth of Violet. It shows a homely little girl sitting in a field of lavender and purple flowers. Gilbert asked if the artist was still alive. It was the best thing he had seen since Arthur Rackham, he said. Vera produced copies of *Fish with Feathers* and *Snow White and Rose Red*. Thus the girl illustrator met Gilbert Seigh one rainy midmorning. He skimmed through my portfolio, and since there was nothing at stake, I felt free to dislike him. I felt he was cavalier with my work. I felt I had been set up by the Martins to meet an available man whose tastes were similar to my own. He closed the portfolio and began to hum happily, at which point I figured him for a moron.

" 'My heart is like a singing bird,' " he sang.

My reactions were coming thick and fast now. I thought he

was arrogant, insolent, pretentious, and unattractively eccentric. I picked up the portfolio and tied its ribbons.

I said, "Thank you for seeing me," and began to leave.

"Oh, wait," he said. "I've put you off. I'm terribly sorry. You think I haven't paid proper attention to your work, but I already know your work. Vera showed me your books and the picture you did for Violet. I was behaving like a fool because it's so good. I'm too mono-minded to have told you. You're the illustrator I've been looking for. Please sit down."

I sat. I thought he was cuckoo. Then he described the project he had in mind: an edition of Andreas Capellanus' *The Art of Courtly Love*. I told him I had studied medieval literature. He glowed with delight, and wiped his glasses. He still seemed a little batty to me, but he certainly knew what beautiful books were all about.

That's how it began. I went home, finished my last assignment, and began doing my best work for Gilbert Seigh.

We worked elegantly together. It was a perfect match. He took me out to lunch often, and never so much as brushed my arm with his sleeve. It was said he had been keeping company with a lady lawyer, who had been more or less a fixture in his life since his divorce. So it was to Gilbert that I dedicated my heart. I brooded about him constantly. Being in love with him brought me all the things in life I counted on: a sense of longing, something to turn over and over in my mind, and that clear, slightly manic vision you get with unrequited love. Each line I drew was a dedication of sorts. Choosing type, browsing through books of paper samples, planning and designing, going over proofs with him, gave me an extreme sense of heady pleasure. If that wasn't love, what was?

Well, I'll tell you what was. I had suffered in love three years before, and it had not stopped haunting me. The man in

question was an astronomer by the name of Jacob Bailey.
Somewhere in the heavens is a galaxy named for him: the
Bailey galaxy. It can only be seen through an observatory
telescope—he showed it to me once at an observatory in
Vermont. I will probably never see it again. I met Jacob in
the line of work—the way I felt it was proper to meet those
with whom you will have a profound connection. I was doing
the drawings for a children's book on Kepler, and Jacob was
checking the text and pictures for accuracy. It was love at
once—hot, intense, brilliant, and doomed to fail. When it did,
and we parted, it was with much puzzlement and despair.
Jacob wanted a grand event—something you would never
forget but not something to live with. I wanted something to
live with. A love affair conducted with the same thrilling rev-
up that starts a Grand Prix race usually runs its course and
stops. When the Rice and Bailey show was over, I went into a
form of mourning. I felt that being crossed in love had
changed me, and it had, but my life stayed the same. I worked
with what I felt was new depth, and carried Jacob around as a
secret in my heart.

When you fall in love like that, it strikes like a disease, and
you can understand why nineteenth-century poets felt they
were either sick with love or dying of it. Divorced people
sometimes remember the joys of married life as strains, but in
a love affair just the reverse is true. Since marriages are final
and love affairs are open-ended, you tend to think about what
might have been instead of what was. So I recalled Jacob's
gorgeous smile but not his cruel streak. I remembered the
resemblance I thought he bore to an angel but not his fre-
quent nastiness and its effect. But what difference does it
make? I remembered. My life—my inner life—became a kind
of reverie, and it would not have shocked me had I found that
in some dreamlike state I had created a little shrine to Jacob

Bailey: his photograph, my book on Kepler, a parking ticket from the Bronx Zoo, the little pearl earrings he gave me. The idea of committed, settled love is as remote to a romantic as lunar soil.

Gilbert's taste in music is that of a tin-eared highbrow. He goes to the opera. He likes Mozart. He listens, abstractly, but music is just another taste to him, and not his primary taste by a long shot. To him it is a sort of cultivated white noise, like glasses tinkling in the background during an expensive meal at a restaurant. Well, I can hum along with the best of them, but my reactions are hardly cultivated. Music is not a taste to me but a craving—something I must have. If I find something I love to hear, I play it over and over again. Then I am able to sit on a bus and play a Brahms quartet in my mind from memory, or any of a million rock-and-roll songs I love. Music becomes foreground then, or landscape gardening. It alters or complements my mood. On windy nights, I like to go home, light a fire, and flip on a little Boccherini, just to warm up. By the time I sit down to work, another mood overtakes me. My best drawing for *The Art of Courtly Love* was done listening to the Everly Brothers singing "Sleepless Nights." When that palled, I started on Jerry Lee Lewis singing "Another Place, Another Time." After a few hours of work, I like a good weep, to the Harp Quartet.

The thing about music is it's all your own. It puts you into a complex frame of mind without your even leaving the house. I can relive long moments with Jacob Bailey by playing what I listened to when he was around or what I wept to when he wasn't. It makes your past come back to you, and if you must pinpoint a moment in your life you can say, "That was when 'He's a Rebel,' by the Crystals, was a hit," or "right after the Dietrich Fischer-Dieskau concert." This kind of music worship is a form of privacy, and a great aid to highly emotional people who live in a hermetic state—a door key to the past, an inspiration.

Gilbert and I worked on *Courtly Love* for a year, and after it was sent to the printer we began on the poems of Marie de France. The poems, since they are about love in vain, made me think of Jacob Bailey. I would break from work to stick my head out the window in an unsuccessful attempt to locate the Bailey galaxy. I worked accompanied by a record of country hymns. My favorite was called "The Lone Pilgrim." A man comes to the place where the Lone Pilgrim is buried, and hears someone calling to him. It is the Pilgrim, who tells his story. Away from home, far from his loved ones, he sickened and died. I played one stanza over and over again:

> *O tell my companion and children*
> *most dear*
> *To weep not for me now I'm gone.*
> *The same hand that led me*
> *through scenes most severe*
> *Has kindly assisted me home.*

Since I was thinking about Jacob Bailey anyway, this song made me long for him. I knew he was on an expedition in Greenland, all alone. I thought of the scenes most severe he might be passing through and the kind hand that might lead him home: mine.

These were days when I thought I saw him on the street. My heart jumped; I thought he had come back. But it never was Jacob. I wanted to go up to the man I thought was Jacob and shake him for not being, to shake him until he was.

There were times when I could not believe our connection had been broken. That was love, wasn't it?

All this time, of course, I continued to be in love with Gilbert. What I thought might be a crush had turned into true affection. The year we spent working on *The Art of Courtly Love* had given me ample time to judge his character.

The worst you could say of him was that he was prone to fits of abstraction. In these states, when spoken to he took a long time to answer, and you felt he was being rude. When he was concentrating, papers littered his desk, causing his secretary to wonder if he was messy at home. At home he was messy when abstracted. His bed was unmade. Clothing piled up on his bed in the shape of an African termite nest. Mail, newspapers, books, and catalogues were scattered on his desk, his coffee table, in the kitchen.

But the result of his abstraction was perfection. Gilbert's books were more than handsome; they were noble. His energy was bountiful and steady, and he gave people the same attention to detail he gave to books. Gilbert got to know me, too. He knew when I was tired out, or when I had faded on a drawing and couldn't see what form it was taking. He knew how to make me laugh, what sort of food I liked. He learned to have a cup of hot tea waiting for me at the end of a day, and he remembered things I told him. When we first started working, I described to him a plate that I had seen in an antique shop and that I wanted with all my heart. This was by way of illustrating a point; we were talking about impatience and the wisdom of holding off from obtainable pleasure as a test of will. The day, one year later, that *Courtly Love* went to press, the second cousin to the plate I wanted was presented to me by Gilbert: dark-blue Staffordshire, with flowers all around.

In short, he was just like me. When he was not abstracted, his quarters were immaculate, and arranged for sheer domestic pleasure. He bought flowers when people came to dinner. He liked to take a long time over a meal. I in turn knew how to cheer him when he became cranky and dispirited. I knew he loved rhubarb pie, so the first of the season's rhubarb went to him. But best of all, we were perfect workmates.

The night we saw the finished edition of *Courtly Love*, we went out to dinner to celebrate and drank two bottles of champagne. Gilbert walked me home, and on the way he stopped and astonished me by taking me into his arms and kissing me. I was giddy and drunk, but not so drunk as not to know what my reactions were. He had never so much as brushed my arm with his sleeve, and here we were locked in an embrace on an empty street.

When he released me, I said, "Aren't you going to kiss me again?"

"Sometimes if you work very closely with someone, you get used to working, and don't know how to gauge what they feel," Gilbert said.

In my apartment, he told me what he felt, and I told him. Then we celebrated our first night together.

The solitary mind likes to reflect on the pain of past love. If you are all alone, it gives you something to react to, a sort of exercise to keep the muscles flexed.

I knew that Gilbert was falling in love with me. I watched it happen. And Gilbert knew that I was falling in love with him. We thought we had been fated for one another, but actually we were only getting used to good romantic luck. It is not so often that well-matched people meet. My being in love with Gilbert was accompanied by a sense of rightness I had never felt before, and we decided that we would marry within a year.

But when I worked alone in my apartment I was consumed with a desire to see Jacob Bailey. This desire was sharp as actual pain. I wasted many sheets of stationery beginning letters to him, which I tore up. When your heart's desire is right within your reach, what else is there to do but balk?

I pictured my oak desk secretary next to Gilbert's Chinese lamp, my books next to his, my clothing beside his in the closet. All my friends lived in pairs, except me. I had only fallen in love—love being what you one day wept over in private. What did you do with love that didn't end? That ceased to be sheer romance and moved on to something more serious?

You get used to a condition of longing. Live with it over time and it becomes part of your household—the cat you don't take much notice of that slinks up against you at mealtime or creeps onto the foot of your bed at night. You cannot fantasize being married if you are married. Married to Gilbert, what would I long for? I would not even be able to long for him.

Woe to those who get what they desire. Fulfillment leaves an empty space where your old self used to be, the self that pines and broods and reflects. You furnish a dream house in your imagination, but how startling and final when that dream house is your own address. What is left to you? Surrounded by what you wanted, you feel a sense of amputation. The feelings you were used to abiding with are useless. The conditions you established for your happiness are met. That youthful light-headed feeling whose sharp side is much like hunger is of no more use to you.

You long for someone to love. You find him. You pine for him. Suddenly, you discover you are loved in return. You marry. Before you do, you count up the days you spent in other people's kitchens, at dinner tables, putting other people's children to bed. You have basked in a sense of domesticity you have not created but enjoy. The Lone Pilgrim sits at the dinner parties of others, partakes, savors, and goes home in a taxi alone.

Those days were spent in quest—the quest to settle your own life, and now the search has ended. Your imagined happiness is yours. Therefore, you lose your old bearings. On the one side is your happiness and on the other is your past—the self you were used to, going through life alone, heir to your own experience. Once you commit yourself, everything changes and the rest of your life seems to you like a dark forest on the property you have recently acquired. It is yours, but still you are afraid to enter it, wondering what you might find: a little chapel, a stand of birches, wolves, snakes, the worst you can imagine, or the best. You take one timid step forward, but then you realize you are not alone. You take someone's hand—Gilbert Seigh's—and strain through the darkness to see ahead.

The Boyish Lover

When Jane Mayer met Cordy Spaacks, she was at that stage of life in which all things look possible. She was full of energy and high spirits. The windows of her apartment faced a pretty street. She had begun to teach for the first time, and her students had liked her at once. The face that was reflected back at her from the mirror was more than confident —it was willing. She felt rather as athletes feel when they are in top form. Her life had assumed a shape she found entirely agreeable, and the circumstances she found herself in filled her with happiness. She was absolutely ripe to fall in love.

She met Cordy at a faculty tea. This tea was held for the Humanities Department, in which Jane taught English literature. Cordy was in the Physics Department, but the Humanities tea was famous for excellent if small sandwiches, and Cordy liked a free meal when he could find one. Each Thursday he ambled over to the formal room in which the tea was held, guest of a pal in the French Department. This pal, the sort of well-meaning fool you get to play Cupid in a campus production about Saint Valentine, had met Jane, who was new to the university. He also knew that Cordy was unattached, and since Jane and Cordy struck him as two of the most attractive people he had ever seen, he felt an obligation to bring them together. He knew that Cordy had been divorced. He did not know that Cordy had spent the last four months of his unhappy four-year marriage in almost total silence or that the failure of this marriage was in large part attributable to Cordy, who had wed a slightly addled girl and then paid her back for it. This, however, is not the sort of information that generally falls into the hands of nonprofessional matchmakers, and it was with a sort of flourish that he led Cordy over to Jane.

Jane had just come from delivering a lecture on Charlotte Brontë and she was in fine appetite. The introduction was made as she stood next to a plate of the famous sandwiches. The well-meaning pal withdrew beaming, leaving Cordy to watch Jane knock back seven of these sandwiches and wash them down with a cup of lukewarm tea.

"Are all your appetites that voracious?" asked Cordy.

"Yes," said Jane. "Aren't everyone's?"

Thus they announced themselves, had either bothered to notice. That small interchange might have been a pair of policy statements, and neither would have needed to say another word. Instead, Jane thought that the word Cordy brought to mind was "winsome." He had a true grin, a slightly manic chuckle, and a very beautiful mouth. Furthermore, he was clearly smart—she could tell at once. Cordy noticed that Jane's hair was the color of taffy, that her eyes were green, and that she was a unique combination of style and intelligence. They retired to a corner to begin a conversation during which they fluttered brilliance at one another. They agreed instantly on everything. Jane felt her best self emerge—charm-

ing, passionate, and original. Fate had handed her the perfect
other. In Cordy's brown eyes Jane saw the reflection of the
effect she was creating. Cordy, who before his marriage had
broken hearts in many of our nation's finer institutions of
higher learning, was captivated. After several days of similar
meetings in other settings and one spectacular kiss, the setup
for which Cordy engineered by taking the ribbon out of Jane's
hair, they were inseparable. Night after night you might see
them in the library, their chairs close together. Under the
table, if you were on your hands and knees, you could see
Jane's shoeless foot resting on top of Cordy's sock.

In the fine tradition of romantic beginnings Cordy and
Jane exchanged edited versions of their life histories. Jane
learned that Cordy was rich. His name was Arthur Corthauld
Spaacks. Everyone in his family had a baby's name, a nickname, or some other corruption of that which appeared on
their baptismal certificates. His mother, Constance, was Con-
tie. His father, Corthauld, was Hallie. His brother, Christian,
was merely Chris, while his sister, Mercia, was called Mousy
by all.

Jane learned that Cordy had married a girl named Lizzie
Meriweather and that they had produced a child whose name
was Charlie. On the subject of his marriage, Cordy seemed
puzzled. It simply hadn't worked, he claimed. Jane knew that
his divorce was rather recent and that recently divorced people are always puzzled. So Jane turned to the subject of his
family life and asked him how he got along with his parents
and siblings. To illustrate the point, Cordy told Jane about
the last big Spaacks family outing. Everyone had been married at the time. Cordy to Lizzie, Mousy to Bobby LaVallet,
the no-good heir to a racing stable, and Chris to a Canadian
girl named Valerie Slowden. Of the three Spaacks children,
only Chris remained in the married state.

The Spaacks seniors ran three households: a *pied-à-terre* in Manhattan; the family manse in Furnall, Connecticut, and a summer house in Salt Harbor. To Salt Harbor the family had repaired for an Easter weekend. There everyone fought. Cordy and Lizzie, when they spoke at all, argued bitterly in private. Cordy raked gravel with his father, both muttering about Mousy's behavior in an effort to avoid actually speaking to one another. Mousy, when she could be dragged away from fighting with her mother, quarreled with her father. Mousy and Bobby spent their time frantically looking for a place in which to smoke hashish unobserved. This prevented them from noticing that they had almost nothing to say to one another. Their son, Little Quentie, was knocked down by his cousin, Charlie, and cut his lip. He began to howl and Charlie began to scream.

Chris and Valerie had no children, and they never quarreled. They brought with them to Salt Harbor their pet, a basset hound named Tea. Tea was sick in many places, hidden and plain, around the house, but found the sea air restoring. At the dinner table, Chris and Valerie were made to feel uncomfortable about not having any children. No one approved of this. They sat in silence and watched the marriages around them crumble.

Meanwhile, Lizzie cowered by the beach. She aligned herself with Bobby and Mousy and spent as much of the weekend as she could swacked out on a form of cannabis called Durban Poison, which Bobby had scored from a South African acquaintance.

This lack of felicity was not unusual. In fact, it was daily life to its participants. The closest thing to affection was displayed by Chris and Cordy, when Chris gave Cordy a tip on the stock market and Cordy fixed the radio in Chris's car. The climax of the weekend came at Easter Sunday lunch. Spaacks senior presided, carving the tough flinty ducks, smiling the dim sort of smile you see on freshly killed corpses.

Jane listened to this recitation with real sorrow. How awful it was that Cordy did not have nice, warm parents like hers. Her doting parents took her to the opera on her birthday. Cordy needed salvation, and love, Jane felt, would surely save him.

It was Jane's apartment that revealed her to Cordy. It was small but crammed with artifacts: watercolors, family photographs in velvet frames, teapots, pitchers, and beautiful plates. On his first visit Cordy surveyed the place and asked: "How do you get any work done here?"

His own apartment had almost nothing in it. What he had was either rented with the flat or picked up from the Salvation Army. The Mayers were a family of watered-down German and Dutch Jews who had once had a lot of money. Now they had things. They had Persian rugs, English silver, Limoges plates, and Meissen soup tureens. It was from Cordy that Jane learned the lesson so valuable to the *haute bourgeoisie*: that some people have a good deal of money and almost nothing else.

Jane sat Cordy down to the first of their many home-cooked meals. She made an omelet, a simple one, with cheese and chives. Cordy appeared to be transported. He had never had such an omelet—not even in France, he said.

"How did you learn to cook like this?" he asked, marveling. "When I cook eggs, they lie around in my stomach all day. Yours nip right into my bloodstream."

"What sort of eggs do you cook?"

"Well, I get up in the morning, put some corn oil in a pan, turn the light on under it, and then I shower, shave, and dress. When I get back to the kitchen, the pan is about the temperature of a Bessemer converter. I beat the eggs and put some spice in . . ."

"What spice?"

"Some stuff I found in the apartment when I moved in. The other tenants left it behind. Chervil, savory. Is there something called turmeric? Then I throw the eggs in, and they immediately turn into an asbestos mat."

"It's very easy not to make eggs like that," Jane said. "I could show you in a second."

"I don't have time to think about food," said Cordy. "Besides, no one ever offered to teach me. If I got used to eggs like yours, I might find myself getting used to a whole slew of other things and end up leading a soft life and not getting any work done. Furthermore, I wouldn't be in a position to ask you for another. May I have one?"

The work Cordy referred to was his dissertation. Since he had been a researcher at a think tank for several years, he felt at a slight disadvantage: teachers younger than Cordy already had their doctorates. He felt he should have his as well. This thesis was sitting on his desk, as it had been for some time. Jane suspected that she was his current excuse for putting it off and that, since he was regarded by his department as one of its young geniuses, it didn't much matter when he finished it. She was working on her dissertation, which her affair with Cordy in no way interrupted. In fact, she felt she was working better than ever. After dinner, she sat at the kitchen table with her books, while Cordy sprawled on the couch with his, but although he claimed her apartment distracted him, he also claimed the distraction was worth it. He was happier than he had ever been, he said.

Jane used lavender soap, which Cordy found extremely pleasing. One day she slipped a cake of it into his briefcase and, when he discovered it, his eyes misted over.

"No one ever gave me a present before," he said. He said it

with such a tremor in his voice that Jane did not stop to say to
herself: "This guy has a trust fund. What does he mean he
never got a present before?" She believed it. She believed that
he had had presents before on occasions but not on the spur
of the moment, simply because someone adored him. She believed. Here was a man deprived, and there is no greater
magnet for a generous woman than a deprived man.

The food he ate before he met Jane, whose use of olive oil
in salads he frequently remarked on, consisted of instant
coffee, powdered milk, and dried mashed potatoes. He was
addicted to cafeterias and claimed a fondness for food that
had been warming on a steam table for several days. Jane had
previously believed that people who ate this way were poor
people who were forced to eat this way, but then Cordy, who
was in his thirties, still had some of the clothes he had worn at
prep school and almost all of the clothes he had taken away to
college. He seemed to feel, like William Penn, that if it was
clean and warm it was enough, but Cordy was not a Quaker
and had an independent income.

When Jane visited each of the three Spaacks households,
she began to understand her lover a little better. The first she
saw was the Manhattan *pied-à-terre*. Lizzie Meriweather
Spaacks, after a trip to the Dominican Republic shed her of
Cordy, had retired with Charlie to the country. Once a
month, Cordy took Charlie for the weekend, and since Lizzie
refused to see Cordy, Charlie was trucked in from the country, and the Spaackses' Manhattan apartment was used as a
dead drop, so to speak. When their affair had progressed by
several months, Cordy took Jane along to collect Charlie one
Saturday afternoon.

The Spaacks apartment was small but grand. It looked out
over the river and was decorated in the way of the reception

rooms in foreign embassies. It was full of the sort of furniture you feel you must not sit on—either upholstered in silk or extremely fragile. The most inviting was the couch, but this was covered in a putty-color velvet that is stained so easily by a misplaced hand or foot. Jane stood by the window and watched garbage scows float the debris of Manhattan out to the Ambrose Lighthouse. The Spaackses, Cordy told her, referred to these vistas as "river traffic." On the walls were Chinese prints, matted with gray silk, that decorators feel bring a soothing tone into the homes of bankers and other corporate capitalists.

When Cordy appeared with Charlie, a white-haired child with tiny teeth, Jane felt she had been delivered. But behind Cordy was Spaacks senior, an apparition Jane had not bargained for. He was wearing a business suit that looked as if it had been baked on him, like paint on a Bentley. He looked through Jane and, when the introduction was hastily made, extended his hand as an afterthought. It was a hard, dry hand, quickly withdrawn, the sort of hand that, when attached to the wrist of your loved one's parent, is often a portent that you and your beloved are not going to spend your declining days watching the sun go down and reflecting on the happy years you have had together.

That was the last Jane ever saw of father Spaacks. Charlie was taken to Jane's house, since she had more to offer in the way of amusement. Her collection of lead animals—her father's from childhood—her picture books, and her colored pencils were far more intriguing than Cordy's computer printouts, calculator, or the camera with zoom lens.

The love Jane bore for Cordy was at this point very hot. It pained her to see the flesh of his flesh and someone else's flesh. She craved Charlie. She cut up his sandwiches for him and gave him his milk in a mug with a picture of a rabbit on it. When they went for walks, she was overcome with pleasure when Charlie took her hand or pulled on her coat to get her attention. She felt that she would someday like to be Charlie's stepmother, which, she knew, was another way of expressing her hope that Cordy would be hers forever. Cordy had said that he would never marry again. Romance and marriage were mutually exclusive, he felt. Jane took this to be a reflection of the fact that he had never known any domestic happiness, and she was a domestic genius.

For months they were extremely happy. Love, in its initial stages, takes care of everything. Love transforms a difficult person into a charming eccentric; points of contention into charming divergences. It doesn't matter that popular songs are full of warning—songs like "Danger, Heartbreak Dead Ahead" are written and sung for those who have no intention of doing anything but dancing to them. And while lovers do almost nothing but reveal themselves, who notices?

But as time went on it occurred to Jane that there was something odd about what she now saw was Cordy's cheapness. The coldness that emanated from his parents' Manhattan apartment, the lifeless, life-denying sitting room, the glacial hand of his father, seemed to hover around Cordy. His raptures about the way she lived began to make Jane feel like a hothouse orchid—pretty, expensive, and not long for this world. Cordy's lavish coo of joy at the sight of two filets mignons, whose virtues in terms of cost and waste Jane found herself explaining, made her feel that what transpired between them did not resemble normal life to Cordy. Steam-table food, empty apartments, and family fights were normal to him, not lavender soap, being adored, and having his coffee brought to him in a big French cup.

One night he as much as stated his case. They stayed almost entirely at Jane's apartment, since Cordy's was not a fit place in which to conduct anything resembling a romance. He had had one bed pillow. The thought that Jane might someday sleep beside him had prompted him to go to a cut-rate bedding store and buy another, whose lumpy filling he could not identify. He admitted, however, what any sensible person will admit: that barring allergies, a good night's rest is aided greatly by European goose down.

Cordy had had his dinner. He repaired to the couch, commandeered all the needlepoint cushions, pulled Jane near, and, with his nose pressed against her fragrant neck, announced that she was too rich for his blood.

"I live on my salary," said Jane.

"I think I ought to go to a detoxification clinic," said Cordy. A shiver ran through Jane. Was living well a kind of poison?

"You live in a needlessly horrible way," she said.

"I live simply," said Cordy. "It's very dangerous to become used to luxury."

"You seem to enjoy things," Jane said. "For example, my things. You don't mind drinking good coffee and getting wrapped up in a quilt to take a nap. You have a mania for deprivation. Besides, you don't notice any million-dollar cameras with zoom lenses around here, do you?"

"I don't use my camera," Cordy said.

"That's because you're too cheap to buy film. It doesn't matter whether or not you use it. You own it."

"That's not the point," said Cordy. "The point is that things give you a false sense of life. If you have a nice house, you begin to think that life *is* nice."

Jane said: "Isn't it?"

"Not for long," said Cordy.

.   .   .

Shortly after this interchange, Jane met Cordy's mother. Mrs. Spaacks offered her son an electric frying pan. She discovered that she had two. If Cordy did not want one, she intended to sell it to a secondhand shop. Cordy and Jane drove two hours to the Salt Harbor house to get this implement, which Jane suspected Cordy would never use.

The house containing this extra frying pan was built on prime land overlooking the water. The setting into which it intruded was spectacular. The house itself was rather ugly and was furnished in that stiff, unsittable wicker that leaves deep red grooves in the flesh. It occurred to Jane that she had now seen two of the Spaackses' domestic settings and had yet to spot any surface on which a human being might comfortably rest.

Cordy found his mother sitting in a wrought-iron chair, doing a Double-Crostic in the weak sunlight. She was wearing a suit that held her body like a straitjacket, and when she stood, she had the sort of carriage taught to girls who know that they will never in their lives have to bend over to pick up so much as a pin.

She did not kiss her son. She merely lifted her head toward him, as if to warm up the air near his cheek. She gave Jane the benefit of a look, shook her hand, and turned to Cordy, whom she then led away, leaving Jane alone to ponder the landscape. Cordy was back shortly, carrying the electric frying pan. Soon he and Jane were in the car, on their way to Furnall, half an hour's drive away, so Jane could see where Cordy had spent his childhood.

The house in Furnall was huge and cold. Everything was covered with slipcovers.

"It's being sold," Cordy explained. "That's why it looks like this. Of course, it's always looked something like this."

Jane was given a guided tour. Cordy turned a corner and

identified a room containing a table, a typewriter, and a wood file cabinet as the bedroom he had slept in as a child.

"When I went to college, they turned it into a room to store their tax returns in," Cordy said.

He looked tired and seemed sad to Jane. She wanted to take him into her arms and comfort him. She wanted to wrap him up in all the nice things she had had as a child and compensate for what she imagined was the coldness of his childhood, his horrid parents, the fact that they had snatched his room away from him as soon as he had left home.

"What was it like to live here?" she asked.

"I can't remember," Cordy said.

Trouble in love seeks a proper issue. In some cases it is sex; in others, politics or money. In the case of Cordy, it was work. The time he spent with Jane, he said, was taking him away from his work. She was too seductive—too fragrant, too luxurious. He had changed his entire life to be with her, he said.

Jane, on the other hand, had gone on living as she had always done. Before Cordy came along, she had prepared dinners for herself, lolled around on Saturday mornings drinking coffee and reading the paper, just as she did with Cordy. She had worked on her thesis without Cordy, and she worked as well with him.

He said as he sat at the table, pouring cream over the strawberries: "All this life is getting in the way of life."

Jane felt as if she had been slapped. She recalled the first conversation they had ever had. She had never thought her appetites were at all voracious—they were the normal appetites everyone had for pleasure in life. That first interchange made it clear that Cordy did not feel this way at all.

For a few weeks nothing much changed except that Jane began to feel embarrassed by her salads, by the dish of pears she kept on the coffee table. The attention Cordy lavished on the details of her life was beginning to make her feel not singled out and appreciated but freakish. They soon began to quarrel. The brilliance of their initial affection began to mire down in fights about meeting places, time spent together, and the cost of lamb chops. In the beginning, these quarrels were repaired quite simply. After all, they had started off magnificently. A glowing smile, a declaration, a kiss on the back of the neck could still bring them back to their original state in which they had felt that no other lovers had had the advantages of their fine minds, their attractiveness, the intelligence with which they adored one another. Now it seemed that there was rather more quarreling than enchantment. Cordy began to display a cold, bitter side. Jane, in turn, became businesslike and brisk.

It was soon decided that they should spend several nights apart. This was Jane's idea, prompted by a sincere worry that Cordy should be working on his thesis and a great desire not to watch her brilliant love affair look more and more like a second-rate domestic failure.

Cordy went back to his Spartan diggings, where, with the aid of instant coffee and powdered milk, he began to work on his dissertation. When lovers agree to part, doom is right around the corner. Cordy and Jane were no exception. When they were together, they found themselves constantly misunderstanding one another, and when they were apart, the misunderstandings were further annotated by late-night telephone calls. It sometimes seemed to Jane that these disagreements were manufactured by Cordy, as if to rub her nose into his reality and show her that life was not, in fact, nice for very long.

On these solitary nights Jane entertained thoughts of throwing out every endearing object she possessed; of pouring the dread olive oil down the sink. It was hard for her to believe that what had begun so happily and with such promise was ending in such a small-time way. She remembered that she had once felt that she and Cordy were protected by a magic mantle against the petty-mindedness that creeps into the relationships of others. After all, didn't people stare at them in the street? Didn't their colleagues look upon them with longing in their eyes? Weren't they beautiful, brilliant, special?

It occurred to Jane that this terrible pass they had come to could easily be explained in terms of interior decoration. Can the cut-rate lie down with the dearly purchased? It was clear that it was all over. Her greatest attributes were now her deficits. They had passed some point of no return—somewhere where discount pillows and imported strawberry jam cannot meet.

Their last encounter took place in a coffee shop. They had decided to meet on neutral ground. The table between them was crowded with empty coffee cups and full ashtrays. By this time they had been mostly apart, except for telephone calls. Nothing seemed to work between them any more, although the looks they exchanged across that squalid table were of pure longing. The fact was they adored each other. How they could feel that way when they were unable to find anything over which not to quarrel mystified them both. But there was no way around it. They adored one another, and it made no difference at all.

Cordy said: "I miss you so."

Jane said: "What is it you miss? You miss someone who

spends too much time in the bathtub, who reads for pleasure, which you think is some sort of crime, who spends too much money on food and who encourages you not to buy your ties in the drugstore. You no longer seem to approve of anything I do. How can you miss me?"

"I just miss you," Cordy said.

"But I get in your way," said Jane. "You said I was a luxury you couldn't afford. I told you I pay my own way, but you meant that I waste your time. You think living a nice life is frivolous."

"I adore you," said Cordy. Jane put her head down so as not to weep in public. She adored him, too. She adored someone who had begun to carp at her every gesture, who made her so self-conscious she could hardly get dressed in the morning.

"How can you adore me when we can no longer be together for five minutes without fighting?" she said.

"How long we can be together without fighting has nothing to do with adoration," said Cordy.

Jane's tears ceased. She was amazed that the matter could be so easily put. She remembered the incident of the lavender soap and his heartfelt confession that no one had ever given him a present. What all this meant was that in Cordy's case, actual deprivation and the feeling of deprivation were one and the same. To feel that you have never been given a present is almost as good as having been neglected. Cordy thrived on this form of loss. He had twenty times the money she would ever have, yet not a day went by that he did not strive to find some novel way of cheating himself out of something. She had watched him window-shop, yearn for an item easily within his reach, and turn away. It was hopeless.

She took a deep breath and told Cordy that he would be doing her a real service if he simply got up and left. He sat for a moment, gave her the benefits of his most beautiful and tortured gaze, and then walked out the door.

When he hit the street, tears started down Jane's cheeks. She ordered another cup of coffee, drank it slowly, dried her eyes, and watched a parade of students walking up the street. It was a hot spring day. Everyone was coatless. A few were shoeless. Couples strolled arm in arm.

And then, out of the corner of her eye, she saw Cordy leaning against a car across the street, watching her. She realized how easy it would be to fling some money onto the table, race out the door, and dash across the street to him. She could feel his arms around her.

Instead she watched him back. It all made sense. He was now depriving himself of her. She thought sadly that he was like a cheapskate who loved flowers, who walked around with spare change in his pocket, prowling around flower stalls to get a free whiff of roses and carnations but never buying any.

Such a man might stand for hours outside a florist's window looking at a gardenia that could quite easily be his. But why, he might ask himself, would a man want a gardenia and what would he do with it once he had it? A man like that might get very close to the florist's door, and might even go inside, just to look around. He might ask the clerk the price of a gardenia and know that he could buy seven of them. That gardenia would be waiting to be bought, but not by him—not if there were no practical reason for such a gesture, and especially since it would be so much more fulfilling not to.

Sentimental Memory

When I arrived in Inverness, Scotland, one freezing March, I had it in mind to tell anyone who asked that I was on a photographic assignment. I had the cameras to prove it. I could have further substantiated my claims to professionalism by displaying copies of a magazine called *Wildlife*, which had run series by me on the subjects of wild flowers, snakes, and cacti, but nobody asked.

Actually I was on the lam, so to speak, from my second husband, Francis Cluzens, a petrogeologist residing in San Francisco, and my first husband, Thomas Ragland, a rancher of Despelles, Texas.

My first marriage had been a somewhat lengthy one. My second had been extremely brief. When I left Francis Cluzens, which I did quite abruptly, I felt I needed an alien landscape to hide out in. Actually I needed a place in which to do penance: no one was looking for me. I needed a place in which a foreign language did not have to be coped with; one in which the inhabitants would take no notice of me; or one in which I could take little notice of the inhabitants. Scotland fitted all these particulars, and so I flew from San Francisco to London and, aided by my pocket atlas, picked the town of Inverness. A helpful and informative taxi driver took me to King's Cross Station and I boarded the London-to-Inverness Express. The train was full of Japanese scientists who, I learned at dinner, were on their way to check out the Loch Ness monster.

I checked into the four-star Station Hotel, where I was regarded as an eccentric American woman on the loose. This was made clear by the bartender in the almost-empty hotel bar, who flinched each night when I came in for my solitary glass of Scotch. No matter how many times I sat reading the paper and minding my own business I could tell the bartender felt that mayhem was right around the corner.

I lived in that hotel for five months without having a conversation that lasted more than forty-five seconds. Each morning, to keep myself from atrophy, I beat a little path from the hotel to Inverness Castle and back. In the afternoon I walked across the square and bought a paper. My purpose was to make my life float in front of me unimpeded. I felt that with no distractions I would be able to reflect on my thirty-one years of life and see if they made any sense. I wanted to put myself in order. After all, I was still young enough to think myself too young to have had two husbands. *Two husbands.* The thought of it kept me up at night and my heart seemed to beat *two men, two men* over and over as I paced around.

In June I did what I swore I would not do: I opened the way to human contact. One rainy night as I sat in the hotel bar I was joined by an overheated boy. I drew him like a magnet. His name was Billy McLeod, and he was home from the University of Edinburgh where he studied architecture. He lived across the canal in Fort Marie and was having a very

dreary holiday. He was violently in love with an Italian girl
named Marina who was home in Florence on her holidays.

A study of the way in which people connect in bars is a
life's work for an old-fashioned sociologist. Perhaps it is the
availability of liquor or the wide display of bottles that makes
people smack right into one another. It took less then ten
minutes for Billy to reveal his state of mind to me—or perhaps it is the insane state love puts young men into that got
him going. He began to talk about Americans, but really he
was talking about love.

"The thing about Americans is, they're so open compared
to us. I mean, they have emotional fluency. I mean, they can
speak from the heart, don't you think?"

Since I had said almost nothing, I wondered why he felt
this way.

"I can spot someone who's emotionally open. All the
Americans at Edinburgh are. They think emotionally. I mean,
don't you notice the absence of openness up here? I mean
Americans tend to notice that. All my friends can speak brilliantly on any number of subjects, but they haven't got the
language of feeling. And if you don't have that, you don't
have any language at all, don't you think?"

I thought that this was a very dangerous conversation—
just the sort I had sworn to myself I would not have. I decided
to sidestep the language of feeling and veer off to more secure
topics, like geography. I asked Billy where Fort Marie was.
His eyes opened. I had been here five months and didn't know
where Fort Marie was? Why, it was right across the Cale-
donian Canal. Had I not left the hotel? I confessed I had not.
This piqued him. Where was I from? What was I doing here?

Were I sociologically inclined I could blame my answer on
the row of bottles, the rain, the empty bar, the peat fire in the
grate. But I was lonely.

"I came up here to recover from my second marriage," I

said. "I used to live in Texas and then I lived in San Francisco. Now I don't really live anywhere."

That, I hoped, might shut him up. It did not.

"I think divorced people sit on top of the mountain, so to speak," Billy said. "I mean, it must be rather like looking down from an airplane. My feeling is that love is process. You go from strangeness into familiarity, into intimacy, and then into commitment. I mean marriage. And then you have domesticity. And if that breaks up, you know what the entire process is like."

I felt that was neatly put, for a novice.

"Love is a crucible," Billy said. "I think you walk into it the first time and emerge a finer, tougher, and certainly different alloy."

On that note I felt it might be wise to put an end to all such conversations, but I was not permitted to leave the table until I promised Billy that he could take me sightseeing. He left, and I went back to my room where I belonged.

I grew up in a small New England town, a nice, obedient, dreamy girl. I believed in everything that was put before me: honor, fidelity, and marriage for life. I believed what the Girl Scouts, the Citizenship Club, and all the love comics told me. I had the temperament for all that belief; I was steady. For example, on my tenth birthday, I was given a camera. From that day on a camera has never been out of my reach. My first ambition was to be a photographer and that is how I ended up. I have never taken up and then dropped any sport, pastime, or friend.

I met my husband Thomas Ragland, whom everyone called Raggy, at college. He was sitting under a tree looking mournful, and I took a photograph of him. He demanded to see the print and followed me around all afternoon as I took pictures of other hapless, less mournful students. I let him into the darkroom while I made the prints and learned that he was a homesick Texan. Everywhere he went he carried a bottle of green chili sauce that he dumped on everything he ate.

Raggy was the first person I ever fell in love with, and I married him. That's what I thought you did, and I was constantly confused by the girls in my dorm who had passionate love affairs and then went off and married someone else. Life was a straight line, a serious proposition. I did not see how you got over anything, and I felt it was prudent to take care what sort of memories you constructed. Therefore I had never bothered falling in love until I met Raggy. Raggy was the real thing. He spent a year at the business school waiting for me to graduate. When I did we got married and went to live in the town of Despelles, where Raggy helped to run the family ranch.

Raggy was big and tall and open, the sort of man who makes you realize how the stereotype of the Texan was invented. He worked hard. He sweated under the sun. He had deep feelings about his land. He was kind to animals. Horses loved him. He could fix a truck, grill a steak, and was a minor expert on the flora and fauna of the Southwest. We lived in a stone house on the western end of the property. Each year we gave a barbecue and fed the county. In the winter we went to Houston to socialize. Each spring we took two weeks off and went to Mexico.

In our marriage we were like a pair of pioneers. Everything we learned about the terrain we learned from one another. We were as fresh and intent as explorers. We believed in the same things. Raggy believed in closeness to the land. I believed in the wonder of nature. We believed that differences could be talked about and fixed; that the best cure for melan-

choly was a long walk; that fights were best repaired by cups
of hot chocolate followed by an afternoon in bed. In short, we
thought that life made sense. We felt that destiny was simple:
you got born, developed lifelong interests, fell in love, got
married, raised a family, and then died in your home town or
the home town of your choice.

Everyone around us seemed to feel the same way, including Raggy's Aunt Bettine, who had divorced her husband,
Uncle Clifford, and then had remarried him. It was, she felt,
exactly what her marriage needed. Later she tried to leave
some of her money to found an animal art museum you could
take your pet to, a scheme that made sense to many of her
friends.

For eight years nothing gave me the slightest cause to dis-
believe anything. Raggy and I knew what life was about. We
decided we would have children after our tenth wedding an-
niversary. Then we would put ten years of pure fun behind us
and get serious. We felt we should first establish ourselves.
Raggy would learn to run the ranch. I would learn to be a
photographer. We would devote ourselves to each other without encumbrance. Then we would bring to life a happy family. Raggy would teach our children how to shoot, appreciate
horses, and deal with cattle. I would teach them how to swim,
cook, and appreciate great works of art.

Shortly after my twenty-ninth birthday Raggy went to Chicago for a convention of livestock breeders, and I was left
alone for a week. Around this time a team of geologists
turned up to survey the property for oil. A Quonset hut appeared on the north border, and in the morning you could see
surveyors when you went to get the mail.

The second day of Raggy's absence I went out early with
my camera. It was one of those brilliant days on which you
can see clouds hunching on either side of the horizon—the

sign of a slow-approaching storm. The air seemed to radiate energy. I rode out slowly on my horse and was wondering what I might photograph when my path was crossed by a man riding on a pinto. He was lean and slightly hawk-faced and he had the sort of uncomfortable seat that people who ride English saddle assume in the West. We saluted one another, stopped our horses, and exchanged a few pleasant words. His name was Francis Cluzens, and he was the chief petrogeologist of the surveying team. I introduced myself, and we talked for a while about the beauty of the Ragland ranch. Out of courtesy to a stranger I offered to ride with him a little and show him around.

He proved to be a pleasant if somewhat disconcerting companion. He asked dozens of questions, and when we finally dismounted and sat under a tree I found myself in the line of a fierce, intense gaze. He was, I realized, the first man I had talked to except Raggy—discounting Raggy's father, uncles, and cousins and my family—in eight years. He told me that he lived in San Francisco and taught at Berkeley, and that once in a while he hired himself out as an oil hunter. Then, quite unexpectedly, he asked me how long I had been married and what I thought of it. I told him eight years and that I was a firm believer in the institution. The conversation then turned to photography, landscape painting, and the geology of the state of Texas. Before we parted I asked him, without thinking about it very much, if he would like to come and have coffee the next afternoon. I thought he was someone Raggy would probably like to meet when he came back.

Francis Cluzens showed up the next day, and we had coffee on the veranda. The storm clouds had moved in from the horizon, and the air was wet. We talked about Texas weather, the Muir Woods, and Mexican food. That is, I chatted pleasantly. Francis Cluzens was not the sort of person I was used to chatting with. Unlike Raggy and his family, he was not big, warm, and open. He was not small, but he was taut and full of some sort of energy I was not used to—the sort of energy that is not dissipated by hard work. When an hour had passed he stood to leave and asked if he might come back the next day. That seemed perfectly fine to me.

The next day we decided to take a ride together. Half a mile out the first raindrops fell and then stopped. By the time the storm began to break we were near the Quonset hut in which the team stored its gear. We made a dash for it, put the horses in a shed, and ran inside. Francis bolted the door against the rain. The hut smelled pleasantly of rope and canvas. Rain drummed down on the roof. There was a window you closed with a canvas flap that the wind was pulling out. Francis went to tie it down and when he came back he looked rather stormy himself. He lifted me off the camp chair I was sitting on and took me into his arms. Not long after that I committed adultery on my husband's property.

When Raggy came back I realized how easy it is to conduct what is called normal life. One indiscretion doesn't do much damage these days. Women's magazines report that their readers fantasize about men other than their husbands during the act of love, but I never did. In fact, I could very well have thought that nothing had happened to me, and had I gathered around me my mother and my friends, and even Raggy's mother, and explained the situation to them, their advice would have been to shut up and carry on. After all, I loved Raggy, didn't I? I had hardly betrayed him, if you believe that betrayal has in it a component of premeditation. My feelings for Raggy had not in fact changed one whit. I had changed.

I was, I discovered, capable of adultery. Before Francis

Cluzens that notion was as remote to me as Jupiter, and a contemplation of it would have been as random and uninformed as speculation about life on other planets. No matter what psychological journals tell you about personal growth, finding a hidden part of your nature is quite unpleasant. It is like being in a war in which unpredictable bullets fly at you from hidden corners. The woman who believed in faithfulness, who thought that life was a straight line, who married the only man she had ever loved, had given herself over intimately to another. That meant something.

First of all, I knew I must have undergone some profound change, or my meeting with Francis Cluzens could not have happened. But when had this change taken place? Had I slept through it? Had it crept up on me in such minimal stages that I could not know it? And if I had changed, I was therefore not the person Raggy had married. Second of all, I was highminded. I believed that actions of the flesh are sacred. I thought I believed in married love, and only married love. I had not been a scared virgin when I married Raggy, but a determined one. Why be intimate casually? was my motto. My encounter with Francis Cluzens shattered all these principles. How casual had that encounter really been? Had I planned it without knowing it? Had I broadcast something to him—lust? desire? boredom? Did strangers on your husband's land ask you how you felt about marriage as a matter of course?

I could not believe that this was whim. If it was whim—pure accident, or a mistake—then I was not myself. Events do change everything. Two weeks later I found a letter from Francis Cluzens in my mailbox. It said that he had wanted me at first sight. It said: "When you are ready, call me. I'll be waiting." On the bottom was his San Francisco telephone number. *When you are ready.* Did those intense eyes of his peer through my good-wife front right down to the heart of a woman who was about to be ready?

A month later I left Raggy. I told him everything. He was hurt, but not in the normal way. He said he knew I would come back. I expect I knew it, too. He seemed to feel that this was something I had to do, which made me realize how shocking it is when someone takes you up on what you think you are. I thought I was the least casual woman alive. Raggy thought so too. He was as he always was: big, open, generous, and kind. He gave me my head as you give a horse his head. The horse goes off in the wrong direction out of some impulse of its own. Then it comes back to you.

I married Francis Cluzens for reasons that probably wouldn't have washed with anyone. The fact is, it was a gesture. It was my strike on the side of seriousness. It was my way of making concrete what might have been a moment's weakness. But I did not believe in the weakness of the moment. It was for people like me that the phrase "there are no accidents" was created.

Raggy was very kind about the divorce. He managed to keep it quiet in Despelles—to make it easier when I eventually got back. I had a man I had left who loved me, and a man to go to who loved me. I stood in a little church in San Francisco, realizing that on two separate occasions I had vowed to two different men to love, honor, and cherish till death us did part.

The trouble with second marriages is rather like the trouble with new shoes: they don't fit the way your old ones did. They pinch in places you are not used to feeling pinched in. All those easy moments, the private codes, the nicknames, the easy patterns, are gone from you. Of course, I was entirely wrong to marry Francis Cluzens. Marrying out of principle is hardly a wise move. And while he was difficult to live with,

my experience of being married to him was not entirely unpleasant. Rather it was continually exotic. Francis was cool
and private. He did not have a big generous hand. He had a
precise, methodical way of doing things. He left his hairbrush
and toothbrush lying next to each other on the bathroom
counter at night. He ate the same breakfast every day. His
desk, when he finished working at night, was neat and bare.
These things touched me in the way that arrangements in
foreign countries touch you. When I said "my husband" it
was Raggy I meant, not Francis. I stayed with Francis for a
year. He was more like romance than like marriage. In marriage you get used to things. In romance what you want is
constant strangeness.

I didn't have much to pack. Most of my things I had left
with Raggy, which gave him excellent reason to assume that I
was coming back to remarry him, as Aunt Bettine had Uncle
Clifford. I thought that I would eventually go back to Raggy.
He didn't seem to mind the idea of some profound change in
me, but I did. If I was going to go back I felt I needed a little
taste of flight, some self-imposed solitude. *I* minded changing.
The very least I could do was to catch up with myself.

Billy McLeod became my tour guide and cruise director.
He took me to lunch at an inn in his home town. He drove me
to Urquhart Castle on Loch Ness. He drove me to look at Ben
Nevis, the highest point in the British Isles, and was constantly angry that I never brought my camera along.

On these excursions Billy talked about his girlfriend,
Marina. He described her as Botticellian, which I took to be
the sort of hyperbole used by youthful romantics, but he
showed me her photograph and I saw that he was only being
accurate. He told me that they had made a pact to write to

each other only by candlelight, and to this end Billy carried a
candle stub in his back pocket so that if the mood struck him
away from home, he could honor the pact and the impulse at
the same time. Their last night together had been conducted
by candlelight, he said, an all-night candle-lit vigil.

He said: "When I think of Marina I get this sort of dream
picture of her asleep. She sleeps with her hands tucked under
her cheek like a little child. Sometimes I can't bear it that she
dreams. I mean, I don't know her when she dreams or what
she dreams about. There's a sort of exquisite intimacy that
isn't possible but which one aspires to. Isn't it sad, sleep, when
you love somebody?"

I found this impossible to answer.

"Don't you think?" Billy said.

I realized that there were times when the only appropriate
response to Billy would have been to strangle him.

I said: "I'm too old to know what you're talking about."

"Too old! My God, I'm too young. I mean, love is like a
voyage and this is my first time out. I mean, you ripen as you
travel through it. I'm just an infant but when I'm thirty I'll
know things I don't know now. Like pathos and heartbreak.
Those are things worth knowing."

I said I did not believe that he would find pathos and heartbreak all that rewarding.

"Well, that's what most people think, but most people are
stupid. Love isn't all jolly laughs and good times in bed. You
have to ripen it. Pain ripens it. But of course the only pain I
know is the pain of separation."

These rides made me long for my hotel room, the only
place I felt I belonged, except with Raggy whom I felt I no
longer deserved. Once a month he wrote to me—a long,
newsy letter to keep me up-to-date, as if I were on some
pleasant journey. These letters filled me with anguish and

gratitude. Somewhere life was going on in a straight line. Francis, on the other hand, had fired off a barrage of angry letters during my first three months in Scotland, telling me what I appeared to be: witless, destructive, and cavalier. Finally, I got a letter from his lawyer informing me that I was being divorced on grounds of abandonment.

Meanwhile, I was losing strength. I wasn't finding out anything at all. My life floated before my eyes and underneath those visions of moral right, of constancy, of fidelity, was simply a person who had fallen into sin. No lessons of seriousness or purpose were being revealed to me. I had acted out of whim, and since that was a notion I could not bear I had let the whole thing get out of hand. Perhaps heartbreak and pathos do ripen love. Perhaps nothing had ever happened to challenge me, and so I had made it happen. Perhaps I had been a terrific prig, holding the world at bay to spare myself the sight of an ordinary mortal—myself—doing mortal things that don't make sense. I had nothing to offer. I only wanted to go home.

I wrote to Raggy and told him how I felt. He wrote to say that I was the same woman he had married and would always be. We agreed to meet in New York to have some time alone, since I feared going back to Despelles. But then Raggy's clan was much freer about human action than I was. Hadn't they understood Aunt Bettine's animal art museum and her divorce and remarriage to Uncle Clifford?

The last day I spent in Inverness I spent with Billy. He took me on a picnic. His mother had packed us a lunch. She was terrifically upset about him. She felt he was too young to be in love, and if he was in love why did it have to be with a foreigner? And if a foreigner, why an Italian? To express her feelings of loss and pain, and to rope her son closer to her side, she went on baking binges and fed him the results. These he shared with me on our picnic. You could taste that woman's oppressive hand in everything she baked. Her shortbread was so intensely sweet it sent a ring of pain through your molars. She baked a black bun you could have shattered a window with. I brought some oranges that I peeled and fed to Billy while he drove.

After an hour's drive we reached our picnic spot—a ruined church and graveyard near a stream. We spread out our blanket in the cemetery. The newest grave was 200 years old.

Billy was radiant. "Why didn't you bring your camera? This is our last day together. I want to remember everything. Sometimes I feel that life opens up like those Japanese fans with pictures on them. Everything seems so beautiful and intense. I hate it that we live from one minute to the next. I want to keep everything. I don't want the minutes to fly away. I want to keep every second intact in my mind."

He yawned and stretched, and fell back onto the blanket with a happy smile. A few minutes later he was asleep.

That happy boy had had his lunch. Full of the moment he went off to sleep as easily as a cat. I looked over at him and felt a pang of something—either tenderness or rage, I didn't know which. I realized that it was occurring to me to seduce him. That's what happens when you go out into the world: you discover yourself in the grip of feelings you did not know you owned. I wanted to seduce him and streak him with confusion and disorder as clearly as a disappointed lover mutilates a tree with the initials of the girl who turned him down. I could show him a thing about heartbreak and pathos and send him back to Marina marked for life—by me.

Of course, he would learn his lesson. If I met him by chance in an airport in ten years he would barely remember me. Or if he did, he would show me a picture of his wife and it would not be Marina. He would have dozens of Marinas.

I took a walk to the stream and sat beside it, watching the water rush past. Above me was a big, blue Scottish sky, crowded with bright clouds. I was going home. Someday all of this would be something to remember. I had books of photographs of Raggy and not one of Francis Cluzens. I had been careful never to take his picture. Certain things should never be captured—they ought to stay in your memory and serve as a sharp edge of broken glass to cut yourself on.

How lucky Billy was to have such tidy notions. Love *was* process to him. A vision such as his incorporated everything, even a random event that, if it happened to him, he would doubtless like to stretch out endlessly. Could you live if you remembered everything, or live properly if you remembered nothing at all?

When I got back Billy woke up and rubbed his eyes. He yawned, revealing the tender pink inside of his mouth. How happy he was! He was out in the countryside with a divorced American woman who was returning to her first husband; who wore her hair in a chignon; who carried a silk scarf and who had been through the fiery crucible and emerged on top of the mountain, a finer alloy.

He took my hand and walked me around the graveyard. Near the church's ruined wall was a crypt. He tugged my hand, and we sat down beside it. From his back pocket he took his candle stub, lit it with my cigarette lighter, and placed it on the crypt. From his pocket he drew a sheet of airmail paper and a pen. He leaned against me. Like most people who have been asleep, he smelled warm and sweet.

"Can you hand me my Italian dictionary?" he said. "It's in my jacket pocket."

As he wrote he leaned closer to me. From time to time he looked at me and smiled as if we were soul mates.

The little candle flickered on the crypt. I looked over his

shoulder and with the remnants of my college Italian I could
make out:

Dear One:
This is a beautiful moment in my life. I am so close to
you I do not have to count the hours until we are to-
gether. We are as near as two people ever were. Each
breath I take is yours. These moments are printed on my
heart forever.

A Girl Skating

I grew up in the shadow of a great man—James Honnimer, the famous American poet. My family lived on a college campus, and Honnimer was its sensation. His classes had to be divided into sections; his readings caused traffic jams on the local roads. When he came back from collecting the awards he was always winning, the receptions in his honor were held in the chapel, since no one's house was big enough. When he played tennis, his court was lined with students who loved to watch their hero sweat like other men; and when he went off campus, you could feel the change—something stopped happening.

When I was young, Honnimer was always on hand as the birthday-party entertainment. He loved a gathering of children—especially the bright offspring of his academic colleagues. If the fathers would not let themselves be made fools of, Honnimer would. He got down on all fours and growled like a bear. He let children ride on his back, and he swung them in his arms until their heads almost touched the ceiling. He could imitate the standard barnyard animals, and he could trumpet like an elephant. He taught children how to hang from doorjambs by their fingertips. Most of all, he liked to make up stories. At any birthday party, you could find him on the couch, surrounded by children, whose feet barely cleared the seat cushions. His children's books started out as stories told at these parties, and after they were published, he read from them aloud and showed the pictures. I hated him.

I was the only child of two professors. My father taught advanced mathematics; he was Honnimer's chess partner. My mother taught botany, and she supplied Honnimer with the Latin names of flowers that he used in his poems. We were a quiet family. Honnimer mistook that quietude for sadness; his poems indicate that he thought we were sad. So into our house he brought noise: large gestures, fierce opinions, his big laugh. My parents, who were extremely fond of him, did not mind having their peace disturbed in this way, and the calmness of their lives seemed to soothe him. They were not silent people, but they had the tidy, orderly habits of scientists. Their colleagues encouraged their own children to display emotions, lest they suffer from repression in later life. My parents would not have minded a demonstrative child, but I was not one. I was a tidy, orderly child.

The stories I was read as a little girl that impressed me most were stories about Indian children, who did not cry when they were hurt. Instead, they were brave and fleet, and learned to make useful implements out of willow twigs. I was let loose to wander in the woods and pastures that bordered the campus, where I spent as much time as possible practicing to be an Indian.

My parents were bookish, and so was I, but they taught me all the other things they had loved as children. I learned to swim, fish, and sail. On weekends, my mother took me bird walking; and when I could read and write, my parents presented me with a pair of child's field glasses and a notebook in which to start my life list. Honnimer knew all this and found it enchanting.

I was the child he loved best, and there was no escaping him. When he read to a group of children, I was the one he read for. I never sat on the couch with him, but in my own chair or on the floor in the corner. When he came to the house, he tried to draw me out by asking what birds I had seen, or he made up a bird and asked me what it was. In the spring and summer, he brought me birds' eggs and feathers, bouquets of wild flowers. This upset me in a way that I did not understand. It made me uneasy that he knew about my collection of birds' eggs, my shoebox of feathers, and my book of pressed flowers. I did not see why he should bother to know anything at all about me. He was an adult, and I was a child. His attentions made me more quiet and solemn than I generally was. When I did not respond as other children did, Honnimer was further delighted by what he called my "infant seriousness."

Everyone else adored him. He and his wife, Lucy, were the most popular couple on the campus. Lucy had blond hair and wore cashmere sweaters. She often went to his lectures and sat in the front row, smiling up at him. When he ran out of cigars, he would look down at her and she would hand him one. She either could not have or did not want children. The two of them kept three large black cats, one of whom produced a litter a year. There was a waiting list for these kittens and also an unofficial lottery to see who got to drive with Honnimer when he took his sports car to the next county to be serviced. If Lucy went with him, they always left a few disappointed students hanging around the parking lot, watching Honnimer and Lucy drive off with the top down—Honnimer in his army jacket, Lucy with a silk scarf over her hair. Undergraduates fell in love with the idea of them.

Honnimer crept up on me little by little. When I went out with my fishing gear or field glasses, he always spotted me. He was either in his car on the same road or crossing my path on his way to the tennis courts. I became so used to these encounters that I started to expect them. As soon as I saw Honnimer, I saw myself: a long-legged, black-haired child wearing khaki shorts and carrying a fishing rod. I could scarcely take my field glasses off their peg without thinking about myself.

Besides learning how to be an Indian, I taught myself to ice-skate. My parents started me on the college pond, holding out a broom handle for me to steady myself with. As soon as I got my balance, I began to watch the better skaters. I studied what they did and imitated it. Once you get the feel of ice, it doesn't fight you.

When the ice on the pond got mushy or started to crack, my parents gave me bus fare to go to the rink in town. There the townies sat in the bleachers, drinking hot chocolate and kissing. My peers shouted and fell down on the ice. In the center of the rink, away from falling children, the serious skaters worked out. I hung around the perimeter, watching. I did not want to be taught to skate. I wanted that mastery all to myself. The things you teach yourself in childhood are precious, and you have endless patience for them. My parents knew that I skated, but they knew that I did not want to be encouraged or given fancy skating sweaters for Christmas. I did not want them to witness my achievement, or comment on it, or document it. I did not want praise for effort.

My colleagues in childhood were the precocious children of intellectuals—ferocious, noisy kids who learned calculus at the age of nine and were trilingual at ten, sources of pride to their parents. My parents, I felt, were simply pleased with me. They were interested in my pastimes but kept their distance. We had three sets of amusements: mine, theirs, and ours. My father loved to go fishing and taught me to tie flies. In the spring, we trekked to a trout pool and spent the day in water up to our hips, pushing gnats out of our eyes. My mother took me bird walking, and from her I learned my orderly habits of observation and notation. But they left me alone, liking to be left alone themselves.

I would have felt my life to be entirely unremarkable and happy if it had not been for Honnimer. He was studying me. He knew what sort of dolls I liked—ones with real porcelain heads, hands, and feet. He knew about my collection of arrowheads and animal bones, and that I had tried to carve myself a bow from a willow branch. He dedicated a children's book to me. He used my name in a poem, "A Day in Pastures with Bernadette Spaeth." When he came to play chess with my father, he watched my every gesture. He singled me out. I felt that there was nothing worse he could do.

At fifteen, I was a relatively accomplished skater. I went to the rink every afternoon and during the winter to the pond every weekend, always at odd hours to avoid crowded ice. For playing around, I liked the pond. I liked to see trees when I spun. For serious skating, the rink was best.

One afternoon at the rink, I saw an older girl doing a complicated turn. I shut my eyes and tried to duplicate it in my mind. Then I looked up. Almost hidden in the darkness at the top of the bleachers was Honnimer, staring at me. You are the inspiration for a poet, he seemed to say. If you think you are being spied on, tell your parents. They will think you are silly and hysterical. They will tell you how great art is made.

Of course he wrote a poem called "A Girl Skating." That was the title of his next collection, which my parents kept on the table in the study, with all his other books. My parents admired his work and did not mind his writing about their daughter. They knew that his Bernadette was not me but a transformed Bernadette.

There was no way I could duck him. If I withdrew, I felt him appreciating my withdrawal. If I stayed away from anywhere he might be, my absence interested him. If I ever spoke to him, he listened intently, as if my voice revealed some new side of my nature. Everywhere I turned, Honnimer was there. He was visiting my parents the night of my senior prom. As I came down the stairs, I saw the familiar plume of his cigar smoke above the wing chair. I was only a girl going to a prom, but that prom, I knew, would live forever. If I forget the color of my dress, I have Honnimer's poem to look it up in.

I felt I had another life besides the one I was living—a life in Honnimer's mind—but no idea what that life consisted of. Certain bonds are primitive, and so was Honnimer's with me. He counted on the kind of pull you feel toward someone who has seen you asleep or has dreamed about you and told you so. He made me wonder what he knew. He deprived me of the right to know when I was alone.

His last book was called *The Black Bud*. I had just started my final year of college when it came out. Honnimer had his publishers send it to me. I kept it on my desk for weeks, unread. It reminded me that for three years I had been praying—praying that Honnimer would never come to read his poems at my college. It reminded me of the intense, literary

girls who had tried to grill me about him; of the freshman-
English instructors who had sought me out; of the general
assumption that I had been, and was still, Honnimer's lover.

I finally read the poems late one night. I did not understand
modern poetry and I especially did not understand Honnimer's. The black bud seemed to be a young girl. In the title
poem, as I understood it, the poet took the bud home with
him and kept it close to see what sort of flower it would form.
In another, the bud emerged—half flower, half girl wearing a
dress that I realized was the one I had worn to my parents'
Christmas party the year before. In the last poem, the poet
took the flower to what appeared to be a motel, and removed
its petals, one by one. By that time in my life, I had not yet
been in love. I had never had a lover or a love affair. Honnimer's poems made me feel how my legs might move, what
words I might say, how my mouth might look after hours of
kissing. I could not accomplish the end of my own innocence.
Honnimer had done it for me.

He shot himself ten days after my twenty-second birthday.
My parents sent me the clippings of his obituaries, a few of
which quoted from "A Day in Pastures with Bernadette
Spaeth" and some poems in *The Black Bud* to show Honnimer's poetic journey from light to darkness. I read these clippings in a cottage overlooking Casco Bay—I had been given
a fellowship to study flight behavior in young seabirds—and
when I finished reading, I took my parents' letter, my field
glasses, and a notebook, and went down to my observation
point, an outcropping of rocks near a cormorant's nesting
ground.

The letter said that Honnimer had been increasingly depressed. He and Lucy had separated. He began to cancel

classes—something he had never done in all his years of
teaching. When he came to play chess with my father, he was
distracted and quiet. Finally, the only person he seemed to
want around was my mother, who took him dinner and sat
with him. The last day of his life he had spent at the Bergmeister Collection—a small and beautiful group of paintings
left to the college by a tin magnate. Honnimer shot himself
at home, my parents said, leaving no note.

The last time I saw him was at the Bergmeister Collection.
Each time I came home from college, I traced my childhood.
I went to the town rink. I sat in the tree where I had read *The
Biography of a Grizzly*. I went fishing and to my favorite spot
in the pasture to watch hawks. Then I went to the Bergmeister
Collection.

Bergmeister had left the college some Dutch florals, some
English landscapes, a big Corot, examples of the Hudson
River school, a German altarpiece. In one very dark room
hung four small paintings—two Sienese, two Tuscan. These
were the paintings I always came to greet and say goodbye to.
One was a Pietà, one of a Crucifixion. Two were Nativities.
In these the baby Jesus looked elderly, and Mary looked
childlike beside him. All four paintings were framed in gilt
and lighted by brass lamps. The figures were painted on back-
grounds of gold leaf. Each figure had a halo of worked gold.
If you looked at these paintings for a while, the room around
you appeared to take on the texture of black velvet. You had
to blink to get the gold out of your eyes. You turned away,
into that black velvet, and waited for another painting to
gleam at you out of the darkness.

I was standing in front of the Pietà, gazing at the stylized,
grief-stricken faces, which never looked to me like the faces of
real people until I moved close enough to see the tiny details,
like the teardrop on Mary's face. I turned away, toward one

of the Nativities, and realized that someone was standing next to me. It was Honnimer.

"They're my favorites, too," he said.

I could barely see him. My eyes would not adjust to the darkness. My heart sounded very loud to me, and the tips of my fingers were suddenly cold.

Slowly he took shape: his long, fine nose; his oval eyes, which in the light were hazel; his crisp mane of hair and beard. He was very near me. I could smell the spice that cigar smoke leaves on clothes, and I was more frightened than I had ever been. What could I have said? He moved closer. He said: "I know you're going back to school soon. I always miss you, but I keep you by me in my mind." Then he bent down and kissed me on the forehead. He seemed to stand beside me for hours, but it must have been seconds. Then he was gone, leaving a warm circle where his lips had been. As soon as I was sure he was out of the building, I walked home, rubbing the spot on my forehead where he had kissed me.

An Old-Fashioned Story

The Rodkers had a son named Nelson, whom all the world called Nellie. The Leopolds had a daughter named Elizabeth. Marshall Rodker and Roger Leopold had been at college and law school together and courted wives who had been roommates at college. Nelson was two years Elizabeth's senior, and he was a model child in every way. Elizabeth, on the other hand, began her life as a rebellious, spunky, and passionate child, but she was extraordinarily pretty, and such children are never called difficult: they are called original. It was the ardent hope of these people that their children might be friends and, when they grew up, would like each other well enough to marry.

In order to ensure their happy future, the children were brought together. If Elizabeth looked about to misbehave, Elinor Leopold placed her warm hand on Elizabeth's forearm and, with a little squeeze Elizabeth learned to dread, would say in tones of determined sweetness: "Darling, don't you want to see nice Nellie's chemistry set?" Elizabeth did not want to see it—or Nelson's stamp collection or his perfect math papers or the model city he had built with his Erector set. As she grew older, she did not want to dance with Nelson at dancing class or go to his school reception. But she did these things. That warm pressure on her forearm was as effective as a slap, although her compliance was not gained only by squeezes and horrified looks. Elizabeth had begun to have a secret life: she hated Nelson and she hated the Rodkers with secret fury. While she was too young to wonder if this loathing included her parents, she felt that if they forced Nelson upon her and chose the Rodkers for their dearest friends, they must in some way be against her. At the same time she realized that they were foolable to an amazing extent. If she smiled at Nelson, they were happy and considered her behavior impeccable. If she was rude, she spent weeks in pain— the pain of constant lectures. Thus, she learned to turn a cheerful face while keeping the fires of her dislike properly banked. The fact of the matter was that an afternoon of Nelson's stamp collection was good for two afternoons hanging around the park with her real friends.

Elizabeth's friends came down with measles, chicken pox, and mumps, but Elizabeth considered Nelson her childhood disease. As she got older, she began to feel that he had ruined her early years, but in her twenties she realized what an asset he had been. Without him she would never have learned to shield herself entirely from her parents. She learned from him how little it took to please: Nelson wrapped himself up warm when it was cold. He baked cookies for his mother's birthday. He played chess with his father. That, it appeared, sufficed—a very instructive lesson that was not lost on Elizabeth, who felt that beneath Nelson's clean, wavy hair lived a rat, a suck-up, a traitor to all children.

Nelson had an older brother named James. James was eight years Elizabeth's senior, and she regarded him as veritably ancient. James had been sent away to a progressive school for the brilliant and unmanageable children of the well-to-do. Here he learned to smoke, drive a car without a license, and play cards for money. When these traits became manifest, James was plucked from the libertine environment and sent to one of the nation's oldest and finest establishments for one last crack at making him an eventual leader of men. In this setting he drank beer, set off cherry bombs in trash cans, and hung around with town girls. By the time he was ready to graduate, he added to this sort of hell raising a penchant for seditious literature and came home spouting Marx, Mao, and Huysmans.

At college he learned a great many more bad habits, including how to spend money, drink wine, seduce young women, and break some bone or other right before Thanksgiving vacation called him back to his family. In spite of this, he did extremely well and graduated with honors. The night of his graduation he was arrested with some of his unwholesome friends for disorderly conduct and was made to spend the night in jail. This was meant to scare him. The next morning he was released, his fingerprints in a manila envelope that he might know the kindness doled out by the police to young men who will someday be their elected leaders.

Elizabeth was kept abreast of James's evil career by her parents, who said that James was killing Marshall and breaking poor Harriet's heart. Nelson spoke of his brother as if he were some pathetic sort of animal.

Over a game of Scrabble, which, of course, Nelson was winning, he commented on the arrest.

"Poor Daddy and Mother. Jimmy got arrested, you know. They gave him back his fingerprints, but it will always be on his conscience, and if he's ever asked if he's been arrested, he'll have to say yes."

"Why will he?" Elizabeth said.

"Because it's true," said Nelson. "Besides, it's adolescent and silly. It's just as easy not to get arrested as to get arrested." Nelson at the time was almost sixteen. He was a nice-looking, somewhat expressionless boy whom Elizabeth found more and more repulsive. All his clothes were clean. His hair was combed. Elizabeth knew that he underlined passages in books, a habit she found disgusting. When he read, he sat upright in his leather chair, under proper light with his book held at a proper angle. Elizabeth, who read under the covers with a flashlight, found his posture disgusting as well.

After a brief contemplation of the Scrabble board, Nelson made an ingenious play using the word "vugh," about which Elizabeth was doubtful but did not challenge. It was pointless to challenge Nelson. He was all-knowing and he never cheated. In fact, one of Harriet Rodker's favorite stories about him concerned a point of honor. Nelson, at seven, told his father that he had stolen two gum erasers from Mrs. Williamson's candy store. His father advised him to take them back. "But I can't," Nelson had said. "I was so upset about stealing them that I threw them away." Marshall Rodker then asked his son how he intended to make reparation—*if*, of course, was never at issue. Nelson had said, "I'll go to Mrs. Williamson and tell her what I did and pay her." This he did, and Mrs. Williamson swore she never knew a better boy than Nelson Rodker. Elizabeth was sure this was a true story but for one detail. She was certain that Nelson had not thrown the erasers away; she knew that he had eaten them. She was convinced that when his parents were out he made mashed potatoes from the *Joy of Cooking* so that he could eat them with his hands.

Nelson and Elizabeth went to brother-and-sister schools where Nelson distinguished himself. He won the Latin prize, the good citizen's award, the math medal, and scholar of the year. Meanwhile, James Rodker had dropped out of what little sight he permitted his parents by going to England, where it was thought he was studying economics or history. Only the Leopolds knew how scanty information was about James. At dinner parties his name and the subject of economic history were twined, but during Rodker-Leopold bridge games all was revealed. As Elizabeth stood with her ear to the library door, she learned that whenever the Rodkers went to London to see him, they found that he had just gone abroad, or, if he was in town, he turned up with Hindu or Oriental girls who were clearly his mistresses. Elizabeth longed for these bridge parties. James's career filled her with admiration. With Nelson constantly held over her head, it was hard for her not to have outright affection for anyone who behaved like a punk.

The beautiful daughters of the nervous well-to-do are tended like orchids, especially in a city like New York. Elizabeth was not allowed to take a public bus unaccompanied until she was thirteen. Her friends were carefully picked over. The little O'Connor girl was common; that her father had won a Pulitzer prize was of no matter. The little Jefferson boy was colored. It made no difference that his father was a diplomat. And so on. The only one of Elizabeth's friends Mrs. Leopold approved of was Holly Lukas, whose mother was an old friend. Holly was the only one to be dignified by a first name. Thus, Elizabeth never brought her real friends home, since, with the exception of Holly, they were all wrong: the children of broken homes, the sons and daughters of people with odd political or religious preferences or of blacklisted movie producers. Elizabeth learned the hard way that these children would not be made comfortable in her house. This might have put a crimp in Elizabeth's social life except that none of her friends wanted to entertain at home. They knew early on that the best place to conduct a private life was in public.

And then there was the Fifield Riding Academy incident. Like most girls her age, Elizabeth became horse crazy. She did not want to share this passion with her parents, who felt riding once a week was quite enough, so she made a deal with the stable that, in exchange for a free lesson, she would muck out the stalls on Tuesdays. This, however, was not known by her mother, who had her expensively outfitted. These riding clothes Elizabeth carried in a rucksack along with her real riding clothes—an old pair of blue jeans and a ratty sweater.

It was soon discovered that Elizabeth was coming home late one extra afternoon each week stinking of horse. She was made to remove her jodhpurs at the service entrance and, when these garments were found to be relatively horseless, a search was made and the offending blue jeans rooted out. Mrs. Leopold then sat down to question her daughter. Elizabeth was mute. One word about manure, and her riding days were over. But manure was not on Mrs. Leopold's mind and, in fact, when she learned that her spotless baby spent one weekday in the company of a pitchfork, she was much relieved.

She said, "Who works at the stable?"

Elizabeth said, "You know. Mr. Fifield. That girl, Franny Hatch, and some boys."

"What *boys?*"

"Oh, you know. Douglas Fifield and Buddy, the one who takes the little kids around the ring."

The questioning continued until Mrs. Leopold finally asked what she was really after. "Did this Douglas or this Buddy ever try to touch you?"

Elizabeth was fourteen at the time, and it was clear that boys were not what worried Mrs. Leopold. It was Elizabeth herself. What wanton impulse would lead a girl to spend her time working in a stable?

Besides, parents of the time believed in companionship with their children. When Elizabeth discovered bird walking or skating, stationery embossed with birds or skates was ordered in case she wished to write to her relatives. This invasion of privacy, which radical students would later call co-option, looked harmless and well-meant and was practiced by most parents.

When Elizabeth went to college, she had her first taste of freedom. While similarly restrained girls went wild, Elizabeth reveled in being left alone and staying up late at night reading anything she liked. The Leopolds were not against reading, but Elizabeth's reading habits contributed to eyestrain and bad posture and, besides, all that reading made one lopsided. One must also sail, dress well, speak a foreign language, and be good at tennis. Since Elizabeth had never had the luxury to read undisturbed in her own house, she had little time at college to drink to excess or become promiscuous.

At home on holidays she was correctness itself. At twenty, in the middle of her first love affair, she was grown up enough to restrain herself from calling her beloved in Vermont, lest her parents find him on the telephone bill. Elizabeth's parents set great store on adult behavior. Had they known what sort of adult Elizabeth had become, great would have been their dismay. Elizabeth smiled beautifully and behaved in a flawless manner.

Her mother was not entirely happy. She felt, as mothers will, that her daughter was not telling her the sort of things a daughter ought. She was vexed that Elizabeth was far away and none of her college chums could be conned. Mrs. Leopold knew she would have to wait for something to break: Elizabeth would want to go abroad to study, or to go to Africa, or she would turn up engaged to an awful boy. But Elizabeth did none of these things. She was graduated from college, came back to New York, and got a job.

Her decision to live in New York was not easily come by, but she loved New York and she wanted to enjoy it finally on her own terms. She went to her father's bank, and using as collateral a diamond-and-sapphire bracelet left to her by her grandmother, she borrowed enough money to rent an apartment on a little street in Greenwich Village and live until she had a salary. Through a friend of the O'Connor girl's Pulitzer-prize-winning father, she found a job at a publishing company and went to work.

Her parents were puzzled by this. The daughters of their friends were announcing their engagements in the *Times*, and those who joined the Peace Corps or had gone to graduate school were filed under the heading of "Useful Service," as if they had entered convents or dedicated themselves to the poor, following the example of Jane Addams, who had after all come from a nice, rich family. Elizabeth further puzzled them by refusing to take a cent of their money, although Mrs. Leopold knew the truth: what you dole out to the young binds them to you. To have Elizabeth owing nothing was disconcerting, to say the least.

To even up the side, she called Elizabeth to see if she was comfortable in her little cramped apartment that doubtless had insufficient heat. In the summer she was sure Elizabeth was suffocating and offered an air conditioner. She worried that the cleaners in that part of town did shoddy work and brooded to Elizabeth about what young girls had for dinner.

Elizabeth was in a state of bliss. She could flop down on her bed with no lecture notes or required texts and read. Her friends, who had discovered many dangerous and exotic ways in which to cherish their freedom, found Elizabeth a little pathetic in this respect, but having the power to read what she liked was the ultimate liberty. Staying up all night exhausted her. Drink made her dizzy, drugs either disoriented her or made her sick, and she did not have a promiscuous nature. She did, however, have a lover.

The lover was her next-door neighbor, Roy Wayne Howard, a large man with an Edwardian moustache. Roy was from central Ohio, and he was a fund raiser for the Center for Union Democracy. To this end he tried to hustle money. He found lawyers willing to donate their services. He had once been a hooded witness at the trial of some goons who had threatened an insurgent rank and file. Elizabeth, who was crazy about him, found him heroic.

Elizabeth had run into Roy in the neighborhood. They introduced themselves at the all-night grocery store. One evening Roy appeared at her door with a bottle of whisky and two glasses. He drank most of the whisky while he and Elizabeth sniped at one another. After several evenings of this sort, plus several afternoons watching football games on television and a meal at a crummy Spanish restaurant, they became lovers, and from then on they were on and off. When they were on, they went to prizefights, to bars, and to the jazz clubs Roy loved. After a month of this Roy ceased to appear. Ringing his doorbell and confronting him turned out to be useless. Weeks would go by until they bumped into each other again and were on.

This kept up for a year. Elizabeth was in love with Roy,

and this on-again, off-again business upset her. She discussed it with Holly Lukas.

"I can't bear it," Elizabeth wailed. "Why does he do this to me?"

"I would tell you," Holly said, "but you don't want to know."

"Yes, I do."

Holly, who was a great fan of Roy's, explained: "For a smart girl, Elizabeth, you have a very selective intelligence. You're like your mother. You like to see a situation in the light that does you the most good. You think Roy is afraid of intimacy, which is a stylish thing to say, but the truth is that Roy is a little too fond of you, and when it occurs to him that there's nothing in it, he pulls back, for both your sakes."

"What do you mean, both our sakes?" said Elizabeth, who was reaching for her handkerchief.

"Roy is wonderful. Anyone with sense would love Roy. But Roy drinks too much. Roy dresses badly. Roy wants to be a solitary hero. Roy told you that his idea of happiness is to go off to an island in Lake Michigan with a transistor radio and a case of Scotch. You will never marry Roy, and Roy will never marry you. Since you're both old-fashioned, that's bound to catch up with you."

"Yes," said Elizabeth. "It's true. And if I hang around with Roy, I don't have to marry anyone else." Holly had told her this before.

"Absolutely," said Holly. "If you married Roy, both of you would be miserable. Face the fact that you're having a love affair that isn't unhappy but will not lead to anything."

Elizabeth knew the truth when she heard it, but still she went to prizefights and to bars with Roy intermittently.

. . .

Meanwhile, once every three weeks or so she had dinner with Nelson so if her mother said, "Aren't you seeing any nice young men?" she could truthfully answer, "I see Nelson."

Nelson called on a Wednesday to ask her out for Saturday. He always appeared in an elegant sports jacket and beautiful trousers. It was hard for Elizabeth to admit that he was good-looking, but he was. One night Nelson, who had been first in his class at law school, mentioned his volunteer prison work.

"You go into prisons looking like that?" she asked.

"Yes, and I wear my watch, too." Said watch was heavy and gold, a Rodker family relic.

"Those cons must really love you."

"Well, as a matter of fact, they do, because they get the services of a first-rate lawyer for free. And why should I change what I wear to go into a prison? I'd feel very condescended to if someone did that to me."

This prison-reform business was hard on Elizabeth. None of Nelson's attitudes were wrong and, worse, he never bragged. How she wished that he had turned out to be a corporate lawyer, voting Republican and talking about the creeping menace of socialism. Instead, he made a lot of money *and* did good works. There was nothing Elizabeth could pin on him.

Nelson always took her to a good restaurant and always paid for the meal, but he explained, "I'm told you're living on what you earn and, since what I earn is about three times what you earn, it's silly for you to split the check. If you wanted to be fair, you'd invite me for dinner. Your mother told my mother you're quite a good cook."

This was a sore subject with Elizabeth. She had invited her parents for dinner, after concealing any incriminating thing in the house. Any trace of birth control was locked away. Any book her mother might pick up and say, "Darling, are you reading *this?*," was hidden from view. All but several bottles of liquor were placed under the sink. No bottles would mean that Elizabeth had no social life Too many would mean that she was either drinking to excess or hanging around with those who did.

Mrs. Leopold, who referred to these meals as "Elizabeth's bohemian dinners," said to her daughter, "I don't know where you learned to use spices in such an original way." Implying that Elizabeth never could have learned from her—and also that spices were common, and that real food, eaten by real people, was either plain American or French.

So Elizabeth had no intention of being fair and inviting Nelson for dinner. She figured he was probably a spy. Still, these dinners with him were not unpleasant, but after the pleasantest of them Elizabeth made sure that when Nelson left her at her door she changed her clothes and went next door to Roy Howard.

In early December Roy Howard moved away. He promised he would stay in touch, but Elizabeth began to cry. Roy said, "I love you in my own way but not in any way that will do any good." Then he gave her a kiss, and she knew he would continue to turn up intermittently. However, his moving brought her very low. She saw Nelson rather more often. He took her for drives in the country, or for walks, or out for dinner. He talked to her about her work and his own. He was an excellent time filler, and Elizabeth began to think of him as an old friend, one of those friends who connects you to your past. During a drive one afternoon he revealed to her that James was coming home for Christmas.

Coincidental with the departure of Roy Howard was an on-slaught by her mother, who appeared one day at Elizabeth's office to take her out to lunch.

Soon Elizabeth was picking at a salad in a ladies' tearoom

while her mother gently grilled her. Why did she look so un-well and tired? Was she having trouble sleeping? Should she make an appointment with Dr. Goldhauer? Did her employ-ers expect her to work herself into physical collapse? Mrs. Leopold had the knack of catching her daughter at her most vulnerable.

"I'm perfectly fine. It's just been a hectic week at work," Elizabeth said coldly.

Mrs. Leopold's eyes narrowed—a sign of war. War had once meant prohibition—of riding lessons and telephone calls. Now war meant a lecture, the only method left to Mrs. Leopold in her futile search for information. Basically, she wanted to know if Elizabeth was having romantic troubles, but since she would not ask, she came down hard on the issue of family loyalty and Elizabeth's lack of interest in the needs of others.

Elizabeth and Holly called these lectures "A Mother's Ten Commandments"—all of which they broke: Thou shalt tell thy mother everything. Thou shalt live very near thy mother. Thou shalt bring friends home for thy mother's approval. Thou shalt offer information about thy love life. Thou shalt dress according to thy mother's style. Thou shalt constantly be in debt to thy mother for sums large and small. Thou shalt have fierce family loyalty on all occasions. Thou shalt ask thy mother's opinion. Thou shalt confide thy troubles in thy mother so that thy mother may become hysterical. Thou shalt borrow thy mother's cleaning woman.

The lunch was not a success, and Elizabeth and her mother parted in terrible tempers.

One week later was the Rodkers' annual Christmas party, and Elizabeth was loaded for bear. Her first step was the purchase of a black velvet dress that was low in the back, low in the front, and sleeveless. Next was the gardenia she wore in her hair. She looked quite beautiful, but her mother could not approve of the dress and she found the gardenia excessive. Nelson, however, found her ravishing and told her so. But Nelson's praise was not her goal: she was after James. She had decided that a little public bad behavior was exactly what she needed. It was time to get her mother off her back, outrage the Rodkers, and put to rest once and for all her imitation of a well-composed young woman. She could also blitz what she considered their tidy plans for her: a safe marriage to nice Nelson, or someone very like him.

As soon as she had knocked back several glasses of champagne, she felt up to putting her plan in operation. This was to flirt slowly and blatantly with James. Then, if he was as dashing as she imagined, she would seduce him and then make it known. Before he went back to England, she would dump him. She was about to edge herself over to him when she felt that warm hand on her forearm.

"Darling, Harriet says you haven't said hello to her."

"Harriet can go to hell," said Elizabeth, so fortified by Piper Heidsieck that she ignored the threat of vengeance in her mother's eyes.

She approached James Rodker. Next to him the healthy Nelson palled. James looked haggard, tortured, just the sort of deep and troubled man you find in novels.

"Hello," she said with a big smile. "I haven't seen you since I was a little girl."

"Well, well, well," said James, "aren't you grown-up?" He turned her around and led her to a sofa.

"So you're Nellie's little pal," he said. "I've been hearing so much about you."

"I've always been hearing about you," Elizabeth said.

"Tell you what," said James, "as soon as the whole crowd is here, let's you and me sneak out for a drink and talk about all we've been hearing. What say?"

"All right," said Elizabeth, though this was not quite as she had planned. James had jumped the gun on her.

But things worked out well enough. They made a public exit on the pretext of going out for a bag of ice and had the pleasure of watching Harriet Rodker's lips compress, but before she could speak, Elizabeth and James were out the door and into the elevator.

He took her to a bar around the corner, a dull, wood-paneled place—the sort of bar you can take your son to after a hockey game. They sat in a wooden booth and sipped their drinks in silence. James lit his pipe and smiled a knowing smile.

"So, here you are. The little number they've tucked away for brother Nellie," he said.

"I am not tucked away for anyone."

"No, on second thought, you wouldn't be. Girls like you play for higher stakes. Love or income, or preferably both."

"I don't play for any stakes," Elizabeth said.

"How refreshingly young you are," said James. "Mother implored me to be kind to you."

"As opposed to what?"

"As opposed to dragging you by the hair, knocking you out, and catching a social disease, or giving you one."

"Have you had many social diseases?"

"Oh, several. I have contracted social diseases in Hong Kong, Saigon, and the town of High Wycombe." He set his dead pipe down on the table. "Little girls like you—I beg your pardon—women like you are meant to blush, or don't you blush any more? Probably not."

Elizabeth realized that the romantic James was rather

drunk. He then began a long discourse on the subject of the
nuclear family, quoting extensively in French from a sociologist Elizabeth had never heard of. Then he launched into an
explanation of the English economy, and Elizabeth realized
that for all that he was haggard he was extremely dull.

Suddenly he stared directly into Elizabeth's eyes.

"Have you the keys to your apartment?" he said, and,
without waiting for an answer, continued, "Give them to me."

Elizabeth was old enough to have been flirted with and
propositioned many times. The men she liked best were
straightforward, brave enough to state their intentions. The
keys James Rodker wanted he wanted to clean his pipe with,
she was sure. The easy way with which he made his request
indicated to her that this was a well-used ploy. If you forked
over your keys, he cleaned his pipe. If you fluttered, James
took this as encouragement and ended by using your keys to
come and sleep with you. Elizabeth handed over the keys and
watched James dig the ashes out of his pipe.

"Clever girl," he said.

"I think we ought to go back," said Elizabeth, who was
beginning to feel sleepy. She was profoundly disappointed.
James was not a man she wanted to flirt with, and she felt a
cold coming on.

"Not so fast," James said. "I'm going to tell you about all
those things you've heard about me." And he commenced to
describe his college career, the flat he had inhabited in London, the girls he had lived with in Paris, the bar girls he had
slept with in Saigon, his position on his paper, and the number
of famous friends he had. Elizabeth had to suppress a yawn.

"All right," said James, paying the bill. "Back to the arms
of the family. Don't you find it public-spirited of our lovely
Nellie to work with the less fortunate?"

Elizabeth swallowed. "Nelson's all right."

"You, of course, are partisan," James said. "Nellie is an insect."

When they returned to the party, Elizabeth realized that they had been gone for two hours and the smug smile James wore announced that they had been up to no good.

Elizabeth spent the next week in her apartment wrapped in a quilt. The cold she had expected materialized. In addition to being ill, she was angry. From Holly she had learned that James Rodker during his stay had not come home several nights and dropped her name frequently. Thus, it was assumed that she and James were up to further evil doings. She said to Holly: "I know I set out to seduce him, but he's just too awful. And besides, look at what he's done! He's set me up! He comes home to rub his parents' nose in it and he used me!"

"Unthinkable," said Holly.

On the afternoon of New Year's Eve Elizabeth was curled up dozing under her quilt. In a few hours she would dress and go to the boozy, happy party Holly gave each New Year's. Elizabeth felt neither happy nor much in the mood for a party. She was brooding heavily but was interrupted by the doorbell. She started—it might be Roy Howard, who sometimes dropped by on whim. But it was not. It was Nelson Rodker.

"Hello," he said. "I was in the neighborhood and I heard you were sick, so I decided to drop by and see you."

This was most unlike Nelson. He was wearing a beautiful suit and gold cuff links. The wind had blown his hair about and made his cheeks blaze. He looked healthy but very serious.

"I guess you came to find out if I was sleeping with your brother," Elizabeth said.

"You're hardly the sort of girl to sleep with Jimmy. He's far too dull for you."

"How would you know?"

"I didn't come to fight with you or to check up on your behavior."

"You came as a kindly gesture to an ill friend."

"I came to see you because I wanted to."

"And to report back to our parents that I'm still alive and that James isn't hiding under my bed?"

"Elizabeth, what is wrong with you? I always think of you as a free spirit and here you chain me to my family."

"You are your family," Elizabeth said sulkily.

"I am most certainly not my family. I don't like my family and I never have. My family is silly, stuffy, and rigid. You're not the only one who behaved yourself and got out fast. What do you think I am?"

"A model boy," said Elizabeth.

Then Nelson did a most un-Nelson thing. He took the quilt from Elizabeth's shoulders, lifted her to her feet and gave her the sort of kiss she had never associated with Nelson or anyone like him.

"I came to tell you that I love you," said Nelson. "I've been wondering for months if I love you because I was told to when I was a child or if I just love you. Well, I just love you."

They stood very close for a long time, the quilt lying at their feet.

"I don't know what to think," Elizabeth said.

"I want to know if you hate me because you expect it of yourself or if you actually hate me."

"I don't hate you," said Elizabeth.

"Do you think you could love me?"

Elizabeth discovered that her head was on his shoulder and that her arms were around his neck.

"It seems to make perfect sense," she said. "But things don't happen this way, do they?"

"Some old friends fall in love, all of a sudden," Nelson said.

"Whatever it is I feel, it seems to have hit me all at once. Or maybe it's crept up on me without my knowing."

"I'd like to take you to Holly's party," said Nelson.

"That's not for hours."

"Oh," said Nelson, "I'm sure we can find a way to pass the time."

"This will certainly amaze everyone," Elizabeth said.

"Only if we tell them," said Nelson. "A secret romance is one thing, but a secret romance worth keeping a secret is quite another. Just the thing for us, don't you think?"

They smiled ravishing smiles. As they stood with their arms entwined, they agreed that it was just the perfect sort of thing for them.

Intimacy

On a cold day in late March, a man named William Sutherland sat in the living room of an apartment in Boston drinking a brandy and soda. Perched on the arm of the chair he sat in was Martha Howard. Six years ago she had been Martha Runyon, an unmarried girl of twenty-eight. Now she was married and settled. The apartment William was visiting in was the parlor floor of an old town house. A fire burned in the fireplace. On the mantel, paperwhite narcissi were being forced in a painted bowl. It had begun to snow—large, wet flakes that fell against the window and melted.

Six years ago Martha and William had met at an archeological conference in the South of England. Martha had been on a fellowship. William was on loan from his university in California, away from his wife and two small daughters. Martha wasn't away from anything. What belongings she had were stored in the attic of her parents' house. She had never lived anywhere for very long—she was used to traveling. The conference lasted three weeks during which William fell in love with Martha and was successful in getting her to fall in love with him.

It had not been clear to Martha what was happening to her. She was somewhat solemn by nature, although life had not given her very much to be solemn about except love, which in her experience existed only as a state of uncertainty, was bound to bring pain, and generally involved unrequitedness, or separation and, in the end, suffering. That it might be easy —as easy as friendship—confused her. No one had ever loved her effortlessly. She had had two serious love affairs, the second of which she was recovering from when she met William.

William was neither grave nor solemn, and the world had battered him some: he had been married for twelve years. He had watched his father and his mother-in-law die. One of his children had almost been killed in a school bus accident. There was something rich about him—affection came easily to him and he was generous with it. The marriage he had made was indestructible, but he knew that he might someday be powerfully moved. He had had several very brief affairs, but the fact was that he had never fallen in love outside his marriage until he met Martha.

The sight of such a grave girl piqued him. She was tall and dark and wore her glossy, dark hair in one thick plait down her back. At first he thought that all he wanted was to see if he could make her grin, but when she finally smiled and her face lit up, that radiance gave him pause to contemplate the laws of cause and effect. He knew what had hit him, but Martha looked to be a slow study, someone who would have to be educated out of the examples of bad experience. He asked if he might drive her in his rented car to a pub he had passed in the next town. It was called The Sun in Splendour—

the name had struck him. It looked like a suitably quaint and dark place to take a girl. Martha, who had attended his seminar and raised some points in it, thought the offer of a drive was a way of continuing a conversation. She had no idea that he was dying to drag her away from the conference and off with him alone.

Once seated in the pub he courted her, but flirtation seemed to drive the possibility of smiling right off her face. She looked alarmed. After several drives, and many hours of talk, William stated his case. He told her that he had fallen in love with her. Her face closed up immediately: he was married. She did not want anything to do with a married man. She was confused and upset by his attention. She was not used to people coming after her, she said. That puzzled William. A smile like hers ought to have caused some commotion, he thought.

It took a few more days, but, after some skillful coaxing, Martha fell in love as easily as you slide off a warm rock and into a pool of clear, sweet water. She hardly knew what she was feeling until she was in William's arms. Once she admitted it, she settled into the first romantic happiness she had ever known. The weather was on their side. They drove out into the countryside. They went exploring. They consulted their guidebook and toured ruins, castles, and monasteries. William was staying in England for two weeks beyond the conference. Martha's fellowship included a year at the University of London. They had four weeks left together. That sped everything up: they were serious at once—serious without any context. They felt that they were conducting their love affair outside time, on the rim of the universe. In that short space they established what courtships are meant to ratify: the ease and trust that come to lovers fortunate enough to find a friend in the beloved. When William finally flew back to

America, they had vowed to keep in contact, and in fact they had written faithfully for all those six years.

It seemed entirely natural to Martha to perch on the arm of William's chair. The cottage he had stayed in during the conference had had one big chair. Each evening William sat and read the paper. Martha perched on the arm of the chair and read over his shoulder. He looked the same now as he did then—a middle-sized, shaggy-haired, well-dressed man who looked at home in anything he sat in.

The chair he occupied had belonged to a great-aunt of Martha's husband, Robert Howard, who was in New York on business. William knew all about Robert. Martha had met him in London. He was an economist and at the time had been working for the Foreign Trade Commission. William knew what Robert looked like from the photograph on Martha's night table. He found it interesting, but sweet, to keep a photograph on your night table of the person lying beside you. He toured the apartment and saw the study Martha and Robert used, the bed they slept in. He sat in Robert's great-aunt's chair and went through the wedding photos.

William and Martha's parting six years ago at Heathrow Airport had been entirely silent. They had no idea if they would ever see each other again. Now, in the same room, they did nothing but talk, although less had changed in William's life. His oldest daughter was now thirteen. Martha knew what his family looked like from the photos he had carried in his wallet. He had a few new ones. His wife, Catherine, had let her hair grow, Martha could see, and she recognized the little girls she had seen the faces of so long ago.

But these things—Robert's great-aunt's chair, the photo on the night table, or the pictures in William's wallet—diminished beside the pure happiness of their reunion. She could not get over the sight of him. That she could close her eyes and then open them to find him made her almost dizzy. It was wonderful to hear his voice.

William had come to Boston to deliver a paper at the archeological society. His seeing Martha had been planned by letter. What could be left to say after all those years of letters? But the afternoon melted away. Martha got up to make William another drink. He caught her eye and smiled. He said: "You still have that old lavender sweater."

She looked down. Had she had that sweater in England? It was newer than that, she thought. She did a rapid computation. He was right: it was the old lavender sweater he knew. William touched her elbow.

"I'm starving," he said. "Didn't you tell me you were going to take me out and feed me?"

"I didn't forget," Martha said.

"Then take me out of here and show me Boston like you promised," said William. "I'm a hungry man."

They had an early dinner. William was tired from his flight. He had gotten off the plane and come directly to Martha. She drove him into Cambridge where he was putting up with one of his former students. They arranged that Martha should come and pick him up the next afternoon which they would spend together. Then William would deliver his paper and go home. William knew her schedule: she had stopped teaching in order to finish her dissertation, but she worked in the morning, and William was committed to spending the morning with his host.

It began to snow again as Martha drove home. As soon as she got in, Robert called from New York. Later that night, William called.

"I don't want you just to pick me up tomorrow," he said. "I've got this place to myself and I want to spend some time with you on neutral ground."

She knew exactly what he meant. What could she do? She went.

The room she entered the next day contained nothing she had ever seen before—a stranger's room. This neutral ground contained two utilitarian bookshelves, a plain desk, a couch, a hard chair. Off the living room, a kitchen with a hardwood counter, and a wrought iron stand that held mugs. Down the hallway, a bedroom. A bed with blue and white striped sheets. A pair of slippers—too large to be William's—underneath the bed.

"What do you think?" said William.

"It shows a lot of decorative flair," said Martha. "Who lives here?"

"Did I ever write you about that student of mine who thinks you can predict sites by computer? Well, it's him. He's got himself a big grant to go to Sumatra this summer."

"That's nice," said Martha. "A few feathers and some native baskets would do wonders for this place."

William watched as she began to pace—a sight he was familiar with. The first time Martha had come to see him in his rented cottage she had paced for half an hour.

He said: "Martha, come sit down."

She sat, not next to him on the couch, but on the straight-backed chair.

"I couldn't have spent another minute in your living room," he said. "You understand that, don't you? In Robert's great-aunt's chair."

"Did I say it was his great-aunt's chair?" said Martha. "I don't remember."

"You said lots of things yesterday," William said. "You sat on the arm of the chair and gibbered."

"I did *not* gibber."

"You did so. We both did. We had a lot to gibber about. But now we've caught up. I have this one afternoon and that's all."

Martha sat still in her chair. She knew she was being looked at intently. She looked as she had looked in England: her hair in one thick plait, her tweed skirt and a heather sweater.

"Everything's changed, though," she said. "Hasn't it?"

"Not for me," said William. "Not after all these years."

"I'm married," Martha said. "I love Robert."

"Well, well," said William. "Married, are you? How interesting. And what does your husband do for a living?"

"Don't be cross with me," said Martha. "Don't tease."

"I think you mean to say that you love me as you love a friend and that any small glimmer of desire you may have had for me is dead. Is that right?"

"No," said Martha. "I just don't know what I'm doing."

"I see," said William. "You mean that I'm an old hard-boiled sinner seeing as how you were a pure young thing and I was an old married wreck when first we met."

"But I wasn't married then," said Martha. She put her head in her hands. Tears spurted from her eyes. What the sight of William caused in her had nothing to do with the life she was living. In her life she was a happily married woman. She loved Robert: she adored him. She loved the way their apartment looked. She liked the friends they entertained, the trips they took, the time they spent together. But her desire for William had hardly died down. The past was a tunnel—a long, dark tunnel you strolled down on your own. Whatever had been between them was not past.

It did not occur to her to hide the truth from William. It would have been perfectly acceptable for her to stand up, smooth down her skirt, and make an exit speech, making sure to twist her wedding ring nervously as she did so. Yes, she could have said, it is just friendship between us now, and if you cannot accept that I must leave.

She knew the rules: if you slept with a man—not your husband—that was adultery, and that was what she and William were negotiating. But this was between her and William. William had some prior claim. She had loved him before she had met Robert, and she believed that without William she might not have known that any happiness could be hers. He had lifted some cloud from around her, and she was grateful to him. After this afternoon with him, she might not see him again for years. She might never see him again at all. What did that have to do with her life with Robert?

"So you're a properly married woman now," William said. "And I'm about to suffer for it."

"Don't tease me, William," said Martha. "I do love you. You know I do." She began to cry again, but William made no move to console her.

"Look here," said William. "It's very simple. We still love each other. We deserve each other. We're both married and we're both happily married. There's still a lot between us, and it's nobody's business but ours. Someone is going to get cheated on—you or me or Robert or Catherine."

It was, in fact, just that simple. There was plenty of room on the couch. One move and there she would be. She would have the opportunity to remember that she loved the way William smelled. She knew how easy it would be—something you could slide right into. It would take a series of warm, drowsy motions to get them off the couch, down the hallway, and between those blue and white striped sheets. And hadn't some ultimate betrayal already taken place? What was the difference between sleeping with your old lover and admitting that you loved him, or of feeling such happiness in his presence, or of weeping in front of him in a stranger's house—a place you might pass hundreds of times with your husband who would never know that you had any connection to the place at all?

"I'd never press you," said William. He got up to make himself a drink, pushing the table out of his way. That abrupt shove let her know how angry he was.

She sat very still in the hard, straight-backed chair. The sky was clouding up, she could see. What sun there was filtered through the stranger's curtained windows. It would eventually rain or snow. Everything in the room looked silvery.

When William came back with his drink, Martha stood up. She had been sitting so rigidly that her knees hurt.

"Are you finally going to pounce on me?" William said. "Or are you leaving? Or are you going to pace around some more?"

"I was going to pace," said Martha. "But now I'm going to make a cup of tea and play for time."

One more moment in that insufficiently lit room and it was all over, she knew. What she really wanted was to get drunk. She wished it might begin to blizzard and shut them in together—anything that might coerce her besides her feelings. She filled the stranger's kettle—a kettle that looked as if it had never been used—and brewed herself a cup of tea in a white mug.

The occupant of this apartment was beginning to make himself known. He had chosen a low couch that was hard to get up from if you were bulky or long-legged. It was covered in some briary tweed that would prickle in summer. The living room rug was made of braided fiber and looked hostile to the naked foot. There was no dust or clutter anywhere. Every surface looked immaculate and resistant. On the kitchen win-

dowsill were three plants—the tough spiky sort you can leave
for several weeks without watering. The papers on the desk
were neatly stacked. This was the encampment of a well-
directed boy who had his hair cut often, who wore a wool tie,
who scraped his face when he shaved, and who thought an
apartment was a place to work and sleep.

While the tea steeped, Martha imagined herself in William's position, visiting him in San Francisco, on his turf.
Would she be happy to be included into his family circle? She
imagined herself sitting in his living room. She leaned over the
stranger's counter and wondered what sort of conversation
she might have with Catherine Sutherland. She let herself
imagine William's house—a black stone fireplace, a window
seat on the first floor landing where she might see ballet slippers, hockey sticks, schoolbooks. She imagined herself being
given a tour of the house and standing at the threshold of the
master bedroom.

The barrenness of the kitchen she was standing in made
Martha reflect on the richness of domestic artifact. What a
good shield a house is, emblazoned everywhere with the mes-
sage that shared, daily life was lived within, something she
and William would never know anything about. She would
never, for example, cook William a meal. They would never
have what must be love's greatest luxury: time. They would
never own anything in common or travel together. Now that
Martha was married, their few dealings were going to be entirely furtive.

Whatever she was going to do was going to be wrong. William was right: someone was going to get cheated on.

But William predated her marriage. He had led her out of
the darkness and into the light. Once in the light, with William gone, she had met Robert. She had liked him at once. He
was tall and rugged and he seemed rather fearless in his deal-

ings with others. He had been a Boy Scout and had never gotten over it: he was genuinely kind and good. Furthermore, he was serious. He fell in love with Martha and wanted to marry her. He was interested in beginning his adult life, and Martha answered something within him.

They were an excellent match. They loved to travel. They liked to prowl around cities late at night. They liked to go to bed early and get up an hour before dawn in order to have a place all to themselves. Once married and settled in Boston, they found that their inclinations meshed. Their household was a perfect amalgamation of the two of them. The life she lived with Robert was real life to her.

Her tea was ready. She carried it to the living room where William was waiting. At the sight of him, her heart turned over. He looked mournful and expectant. For a moment they were simply lovers with a past between them.

It seemed to her the first real moment of her marriage—not her marriage to Robert, but her sense of herself as a married person. She felt exactly divided between the woman she was now and the woman she had been. The world in which she had been William's lover and would be again, the place from which her letters to him were written and his to her were kept—the place in which she now stood was only hers.

William had put on a light. It lit up Martha's face—that grave face he knew so well. What he called her fierce Quaker look was gone. She looked only serious and considering. He stood up and took her hand. She was sure that she was trembling. They walked down the hallway to the stranger's bedroom. At the doorway, William kissed her. She kissed him back, but it would have been more appropriate, she thought, to shake his hand to signify the formality, the seriousness of the occasion.

Travel

My husband learned to love flying in the army. He was sent to Vietnam, and flew over the delta with a buddy. After his hitch, he returned unharmed, but not to me. He was married to someone else at the time, and found on his return that his wife didn't want him anymore. Of this he says, "I created widows during the war, and the war made a widow out of me."

That overstates the case, but he is a man not unencumbered by theatricality when it suits his purpose. The fact is, they should never have married. They were both at Juilliard, and contemplated a life of sheet music and duets. When he went to Vietnam, he thought about the war, and she thought about him. If he had thought about her—if there had been no war he was forced to contemplate—his return might not have been so filled with bafflement.

My husband likes the intense moments of flying—ice, fog, flying on instruments, heavy weather. On jets, he likes takeoff,

landing, and air turbulence. When we travel, we jet to someplace central and then trek through the airport to a spur line.
We have been to Laconia, New Hampshire, on Winnipesau-
kee; Bear, Montana, on Wild Cat; Myra Springs, Louisiana,
on Cajun; Fulton, Kentucky, on Rebel; Mansard, Oklahoma,
on Apache; and Bogotá, Colombia, on El Condor.

We met flying—or, rather, we found ourselves at the same
table at the same inn, having flown to the same place. The inn
was on Tangier Island, a tiny fishing island in the middle of
the Chesapeake Bay with a private airstrip. Our table was full
of aviators. I was flown there—as a favor to my sister, who
felt I should get out more—by a jovial lawyer friend of my
brother-in-law's. He sat next to me while I leaned against the
table and stared at my husband.

My husband is a concert pianist who hates performing.
Instead, he makes records and tries to live like a recluse. He
hates performing because he hates to travel for a purpose. He
likes travel only for itself. He hates hotels, hotel food, and
schedules. When he was younger, he did several concert tours,
and they baffled him the way his divorce did. He felt there was
no center to anything—just a series of cities and stages, and
nothing to go back to. Once in a while, his agent pressures
him into a recital at Carnegie or Alice Tully Hall, for which
he trots out the most difficult or inaccessible music he can
find—his admirers only seem to love him more for it.

His love of flying has made his agent old before his time, or
so his agent says. "Why does he want to chance death so
often?" his agent asks. "It's not the commercial flights—it's
those weird little planes he likes to fly around in."

My husband wants to be weightless, and flying is as close as
he can get to it. If he had not been a pianist, he might have
been an astronaut, he thinks, but he is too tall. If he had been
two inches taller, he would never have been drafted, and

therefore would never have flown at all. After being married to him for three years, I began to fear that he would crash— him, not me, although we always fly together. My dreams, which were usually very ordinary dreams, became crowded with flaming wreckage, torn limbs, and the feeling you some- times have before falling asleep of falling out of gravity, of falling straight down.

No one thought I would get married. My sister and mother brooded about me, but I did not fall in love with any ease or frequency, and the few times I did, nothing ever came of it. Instead, my life was tidy. I had an apartment overlooking a garden, and I commuted daily in a secondhand Saab to a marine-biology station in Riiks Point, Long Island, where I performed experiments with oil-eating algae.

My sister is ten years older than I; my brother is fifteen years older. I was an afterthought, and since that fact is unde- niable I had from very early on a sense of adult sexual life. When I learned at five the way babies are created, I looked at my handsome, stoic parents and realized what they had done to get me. Later, I felt there was something special, something particularly loving and intense about my conception. But the sense of being an afterthought marked me—although I was not an unhappy surprise to my parents—as sickly children or refugee children are marked, and I grew up thinking that I would always be thought of last, the thing that you didn't plan for but that turned up anyway.

For example, when I met my husband on Tangier Island, it never occurred to me that I would ever see him again. When I got to know him, he did not expect ever to remarry, although at the time he was allied with a flutist who had long red hair. He thought his first wife had broken his heart irreparably.

I am tall, wide-boned, but thin. In the summer, I tan easily.
I spent a year at a marine-biology station at Baja, and a
summer at Woods Hole, and each time turned the color of
burnt cork. But in the winter I am slightly yellow. My hair is
my best feature: very thick, very straight—a darkish-yellow
color. For this reason, although my given name is Marguerite,
my baby name was Butter.

The day I met my husband, he said two things that shocked
me. After lunch, we walked around the island, by the shore.
The aviators ambled together, talking shop. I walked with my
husband. At the water's edge, he said, "You have a very con-
templative relationship with the ocean," and I explained that I
was a marine biologist. Then he said, "You look very buttery.
I noticed at lunch."

It is true that you can feel a wave of love; I did. I felt my
heart being torn open, and I accepted it. It was something that
happened without consequence, so I let it happen. On that
particular day, my vision of these matters was particularly
bleak, and I did not believe that any virtue came of chance
meetings or accidents of destiny. But suddenly I felt intelligi-
ble to another person, who knew by looking that I had been
called Butter and that I had a connection with the sea. It was
only a moment, but I was grateful. It is not everyone who gets
a moment of unexpected understanding on a remote island
you have to fly in a private plane to get to.

By the end of the afternoon, we had trotted the circum-
ferences of Tangier twice and went back to the airstrip to fit
ourselves into separate planes. My husband knew my name
and where I lived, and I knew his name and where he lived.
We shook hands as our two pilots started their engines and
the propellers churned up the air.

I never thought that I would see him again, but I did. He
came to see me one rainy evening without calling first, with-

out giving any reason for his visit. He might have said, "People shouldn't meet on an island and never see each other again," but he didn't. He gave my apartment the once-over, and sat in the best chair.

At the time I lived in all ways like a Shaker. My apartment might have had fresh straw on the floor. It was in an old Village building. The rafter beams had been exposed, and all the walls were white. I didn't have much in the way of ornament or furniture, so it was not entirely my fault that my apartment looked like a restored room at the Hancock Shaker Village. What I had was old. I had a glass bird from my grandfather, an eighty-year-old decoy given to me by my boss at Woods Hole, and my father's brass fishing rod, hung across two hooks. I had a watercolor of flowers my grandmother had painted and a picture of a donkey, done by my great-grandmother. I hadn't had anyone to love in three years.

From the armchair my husband asked if I would like to have dinner with him—if I was hungry, that is. His visit was so informal that I didn't feel the need to state anything except the case. I said that I didn't want to go out but that I would feed him.

The food I lived on was eccentric. I strained yogurt through cheesecloth to concentrate it, and I ate it with pickled cabbage and salted Japanese plums. I cooked carrots with honey and garlic and ate them cold—the odd tastes of a solitary person. When I had people in to dinner, I spent days wondering what ordinary people ate. I gave my husband what I ate: a cup of thick yogurt; a plate of pickled cabbage, salted plums, and cold carrots; and some chicken cooked the way I liked it—with soy sauce, paprika, and clove. He ate what was set before him and never said he found the meal strange, which warmed me to him. It never occurred to me that he might have the same odd taste, or his own odd taste. Outside, the rain spun on intensely. My husband said, "I came over here to claim you, if that's possible."

When I looked at him, I realized that I had never wanted anyone so much in my life, so I claimed him, too.

Thus, at the age of thirty, in top physical condition, with excellent training and an excellent job, the author of two highly praised monographs—one on oil-eating algae and one on the regenerative mechanism in starfish—I found myself involved with a tall, standoffish, moody, and temperamental pianist, who, at the time we claimed each other, was living on the upper West Side with a flutist. It was not until weeks later, by which time my husband and I claimed each other every chance we got, that I knew of his alliance with her. I never knew her name. After I was made aware of her existence, there were times when my husband did not call when he said he would, or called to say that he would not appear as he had planned, and I expect he thought that my knowledge of his situation would get him off the hook.

On the other hand, my husband knew the condition that lay beneath that tidy apartment. He knew I strove to keep my life level, and that if he was not around I would work at my research, commute to work, strain my yogurt, and live as I had always done. He knew I didn't want to expect much—I was frightened to. He knew if he wasn't around I would step back and run my life as if he had never walked into it.

But he was wrong. He didn't know what he had done, so I told him, as simply as you explain addition to a child. I told him that I had a heart to break and that he was breaking it. I said I didn't want to be misunderstood, and as I said these things I could imagine how he would look leaving my apartment, and how I would feel watching him walk down the street. But he didn't leave. He asked me to marry him. Then he went home and settled matters with the flutist. Five months later, we were married at my parents' house, and the chief emotional feature of that wedding was relief.

But retrospect makes everything look easy. It wasn't as easy as that. There was a large gulf between finding out about the flutist and saying anything about it—I was that glad to have someone love me. I wanted my Shaker life disturbed utterly but quietly. I didn't want slammed doors or shouting. One night, my husband and I sat down quietly and wrenched our hearts out—at least, I wrenched mine. He went home, and for a week I didn't see him. Those nights, I felt I was sleeping on top of a live wire in a rainstorm, I was so fearful. I made lists of his bad qualities: covert, silent, moody, sometimes won't talk, doctrinaire about music, frequently snobbish, has girl on whom he cheats—with me. I thought I would never come to know him. On the other hand, when he looked at my life what did he see? Did he see some multilayered, complicated homemade jam with a thick seal of paraffin on top? How did he know what he was getting into?

Well, he left the flutist without a trace—on himself I mean. I never saw one of her possessions, or any letter she may have written. One day he showed me a diary he kept sporadically —two years in one notebook, mostly musical ruminations. He lived with her a year, and she was never mentioned once.

My husband had been drafted over the protest of his agent, the head of Juilliard, and several renowned pianists. The president of Octagon Records had threatened to take out a protest ad in the *Times*, but my husband put his foot down. None of this sat well with him—he didn't see why he should be exempt from service because he was talented, while those who were

not talented were unspared. It was not exactly a noble senti-
ment; it was, rather, that he wanted to be left alone. He didn't
have any feelings about the war, but he had been a prodigy in
a mild sort of way, and he was tired of special treatment.

Actually, as it turned out, he liked the army. No one had
ever heard of him, and he sat around the canteen playing
"Chopsticks" on the piano; this ironic gesture amused him.
The war itself upset him, but he was glad, since it was an
upset outside himself. Besides, he isn't very protective about
his hands, as some musicians are. All his life he fought his
parents and teachers for the right to play baseball and otherwise endanger his priceless limbs. In the winter, he never
wears gloves, and he likes to go fishing. The fish he likes best
are fighters—bass and blues. He says he was more comfortable in the army than he ever had been before.

We are not a young couple, so our sense of personal history
is wide and separate. My husband remembers his first piano—
a child's piano. My family took lessons on a huge Chickering
we felt like gnats in front of, and forgot all we had learned by
the time we were in high school. I didn't play Mozart sonatas
when I was twelve. Instead, I stole a lipstick from a drugstore
in Kennebunkport, Maine. My husband was thirty-five when
we got married, and I had just turned thirty-one. We didn't
have a pool of mutual friends. The friends he had at Juilliard
he had either outgrown or known so well so long that they
seemed exclusively his. His pals from the army live in places
like Ketchum, Idaho, or Blue Mountain Lake, New York,
and he never sees them. No, we came with separate friends.
We have separate love affairs to think about. He had his marriage. I saw whales at Baja, and he saw combat in Vietnam.
That accounts for a lot of richness but quite a lot of sadness,

too. I would be happy not to travel on out-of-the-way spur lines—although I love to fly over islands—but I often think the more we travel to inaccessible places the more we will be like a couple who fell in love in high school and married out of college. Our personal histories will merge, and our reference point will be each other. The parts of my life that were solitary will blur. He will think, maybe after thirty years, that it was to me he wrote from Vietnam, and I will think that I commuted home in my old Saab from Riiks Point to him, and my prim apartment will be the memory of waiting at a bus stop before my husband came along to pick me up.

In September, we flew to Miami on a yellow jet, and in a glum corner of the airport we found our spur line, Everglades Airways. We were going to fly to French Falls. The gloomy lobby was manned by an overweight giant with hair crew-cut into a putting green, and a dour monosyllabic Indian with a gold tooth. Waiting for the tiny Cessnas were our fellow-travelers: a Cuban woman and her child, three sleeping Indians with straw hats and dead cigars, a dissipated boy in rumpled white ducks, and us. No one was flying. We sat down and waited out the tail end of a tropical storm.

We ended up waiting for three hours. The chairs filled up with Cubans, farmers, and fishermen. Finally, the flights were called. Eight people lined up to go to Oopalachia. Six flew off to Little Trinidad. The fishermen went to Connaught Key. They all had to wait for the morose Indian to load the luggage and for the pilots to finish their coffee. The pilots on spur lines are like motorcycle racers. Given the chance, they would fly in any weather, but commercial responsibility imposes itself on them. The older ones were mail pilots, the middle-aged ones were commercial pilots who got bored, and the younger ones learned to fly in Vietnam and didn't want to stop once they got home.

Finally, we lined up for French Falls. The plane held eight, but there were only six of us: the Cuban woman and her child, my husband and I, and a couple who appeared at the last moment—a hatchet-faced man with a blond pompadour, carrying a fiddle case, and his wife, whose cheekbones obliterated her eyes. They looked like birds of prey in a moment of pause.

Our pilot's name was Ike Fooley, a stocky vet with a moustache. He knew everyone on the flight except us, but my husband sat co-pilot with him and learned that they had been in Vietnam at the same time. When we got to French Falls, we went to the bar of the local lodging house and had dinner with him. Ike Fooley had been considered the dolt of his family, he told us. His father and brothers were in steel, in New Orleans. He had saved enough to have his own plane. He pulled out a picture of it—a red-and-white Piper Cherokee with *Fool's Paradise* painted on the wing in black. He also showed us a stack of photographs of Hué—the intense, heartsick photos of an amateur. He said that he had still not gotten over what had happened to him in the war, that he was slow and that it took him a long time to sort things out. His moustache curved down and gave his cheery face an edge of mournfulness. After dinner, he told us who our fellow-travelers were. The Cuban woman was the housekeeper at a mansion outside French Falls that was owned by the former ambassador to Argentina. The couple had just come back from a fiddle competition in Paris, Kentucky. They flew around quite a bit, Ike said—to Nashville and Muscle Shoals to do studio work—but they didn't like it much. The man had explained country fiddling to him as follows: "Something pretty you put on the edge of something plain."

As we had our dinner, the weather kicked up, and finally another storm broke. Ike Fooley called Miami to say he was laying over. He and my husband settled down to drink. Ike asked why we had come to French Falls, and we told him the truth. The truth was it was just a place to fly to. My husband subscribed to *Aviator* magazine to keep informed on remote landing strips and oddball spur lines. French Falls sounded good to him, since he was just about to record the French Suites. Ike found this altogether reasonable. But he said there wasn't any reason to stay in French Falls unless you lived there, so he offered to take us to Key West the next day. He had the weekend off, he said, and if we liked to fish and snorkel, he knew a good place to do both. In the morning, we would fly back to Miami with him, drive to a private airport, pick up *Fool's Paradise*, and fly around the Keys.

They stayed downstairs to drink out the storm, and I went to our room to take a bath and go to sleep. The room smelled of seawater and rain.

As I lay in bed, I thought of all the places we had flown to as something pretty you put on the edge of something plain. The love my husband and I bore for each other seemed very plain to me—there was still no communal reference point for it. It was only the two of us.

One day after we were married, my husband opened up a battered wicker case and put on the bed an ammunition pouch, a dog-eared copy of the "Italian" Concerto, a leather-bound diary, and his army belt—his relics of the war, he said. When he pulled shift, he had studied the "Italian" Concerto and sung it in his head. During the sixties, you often saw in slick, liberal magazines photos of the possessions of dead or captured enemies, photos that were meant to show you that the enemy was a human being, too. That clutter on the bed looked like one of those photos, but these things belonged to my husband. I remember thinking, What if he hadn't come back to me? Suppose he had come back to me all shot up? Suppose he had never come back at all? I never touched a thing on the bed—I remembered that I hadn't known him when he came back, that we had met by chance in a time when people didn't think much about the war, and if you said you had fought in it they looked at you without much interest, registering a fact they had no connection to, or for.

In point of fact, my husband takes the ammunition pouch, his army belt, the diary, and that score for the "Italian" Concerto with him whenever he flies. I saw them first one evening while I was unpacking in Shawano, Wisconsin, to which we had flown on Wolverine, and I've seen them ever since. I've never mentioned it, and neither has he, but it is a fact between us, since I always unpack for him.

He carries around those artifacts, and I dream about wrecked jets. Secretly, I read accounts of crashes in the paper, which indicates to me that I never get used to flying, that I am always caught between thrill and fear. He knows I read the paper for those ghoulish accounts, and I know about his kit. But it all works out. When he isn't rehearsing, and I get time off from the Riiks Point marine-biology station, we fly to someplace central and then to someplace remote so that I can ask, some wide, scopeless afternoon on a bleak winter's day, "Remember when we flew around Key West with Ike Fooley?" And my husband can nod yes, with exclusive understanding.

Delia's Father

Delia Schwantes's father did not work. Her mother worked —she taught French in the private school to which we and Delia were sent. Delia, as the child of a teacher, was a scholarship pupil, while our parents paid through the nose to get us our education. Some of us had crushes on Delia's mother, who wore the sort of clothes our mothers never would have worn: plaid skirts with pleats, and plain sweaters like a schoolgirl. She wore her hair in a chignon, and she was the first person we had ever seen with pierced ears. Our mothers, who favored short hair and pearl clip-ons, said that Frenchwomen such as Delia's mother did not need money in order to have style. The Schwanteses, of course, had no money.

There were a number of girls with crushes on Delia herself. She was thin and undersized with features our mothers said she would grow into. We looked like ruddy, well-fed American girls, but Delia with her straight, pale hair and rather mournful eyes looked like a sprite, an elf, some creature out of a storybook published abroad.

Then there was Delia's father who occasionally turned up at school functions but was mostly seen around town. He wore gabardine shirts of rose and blue and brown, with knitted ties and twill trousers and shoes that slipped on— these were the mark of a lounge lizard. Our fathers wore sturdy English business shoes that laced. Delia's father chain-smoked imported cigarettes that came in a flat, ornamental tin. Our fathers, who believed that cigarettes were for women and foreigners, smoked pipes and cigars. For some of us, our first whiff of manhood, apart from the customary smells of our own old men, was Delia's father's cigarettes, and whatever sort of imported cologne he used.

Our fathers all knew each other, or seemed to. They were each other's law partners, or fellow club members, or business associates, or they were related or had been at school together. On the weekends they played golf and tennis together and at night they found themselves at dinner parties discussing politics or the stock market. We had never seen anyone like Delia's father.

He had been one of a group of avant-garde artists and poets in Prague called the Ten Wild Men. He had been a poet and journalist and had fought in the Resistance. Once in a while a review or poem of his would appear in one of those cultural journals, and he occasionally translated books from French and Czech. When Delia was asked what her father did, she said he was a writer, which sounded much more wonderful to us than banker, lawyer, or stockbroker.

Her father spoke four languages: Czech with his oldest friend—a man with whom he played game after game of very fast chess called "Blitzkrieg"; French to his wife; English to his daughter; and German to the refugee tailor who made his trousers and jackets for him at half price. Although he did not consider Italian one of his languages, he could pass the time of day with the man who sold him vegetables and fruit.

He had glossy brown and grey hair which he combed straight back from his beautiful, high forehead. He was of middle size and looked both delicate and strong at the same time. In his direction people said things like: "Never trust a man who dresses too well." Men, by which we meant our fathers, paid no attention to him. He didn't register with them, and at school functions they passed him as if he were invisible. Our mothers, on the other hand, were drawn to him.

We were the daughters of people who had money instead of imagination and complete self-confidence. We came from good Jewish and Episcopalian families, and we grew up all alike. We all had small dogs—but not too small—miniature dogs being for the nouveau riche. We had hearty, solid dogs like Scottish and wire-haired terriers, or dachshunds or Welsh corgis, like the Queen of England. Our mothers lunched with one another, worked as volunteers for charities, and were active in our school. Our fathers wore hats and looked most natural either in bathing trunks or business suits. The kind of clothes Mr. Schwantes wore were unknown to them. For sport they wore the brightly colored clothing golfers favor and always looked rather clownish. By and large our parents' lives were invisible to us—we never saw what they did all day. Our visible adults were Mr. and Mrs. Schwantes.

It was not until we began to get around the city by ourselves that we ever ran into Delia's father. One or another of us saw him on the street, or coming out of a café or restaurant bar, or going into a museum—always with a woman. Vivvie Herbert's sister, a beauty at sixteen, had been escorted by him through the Museum of Modern Art and out to the sculpture garden for coffee. The Herberts did not believe in coffee for children—it made them too nervy. The cup of coffee Delia's father bought for her caused great commotion in Vivvie's sister. She gulped it and bolted like a good girl.

When I was fifteen I met up with him at the zoo in Central Park. He was standing in front of the lion cage, and he appeared to have tears in his eyes.

You did not greet Delia's father in any ordinary way. There was some proper, formal European way in which to salute him. I always extended my hand and flicked my heel in a faint imitation of the curtsey I had been taught as a child.

He took my hand. "Ah," he said. "It is Georgia Levy. What lovely names your parents give you. These names intrigue me very much."

His eyes were hazel, and they glittered like reptile eyes. He lit one of his cigarettes. The tin box they came in was red, white, and gold. How lucky for Delia to have a father who smoked such wonderful cigarettes and probably gave her the boxes to keep her bobby pins in. It was clear that he was waiting for someone. He said: "You must forgive me this moment of emotion. I am very sentimental about wild animals." He took my hand—you shook hands with Delia's father upon greeting and leaving. The encounter was over.

When Delia said "my father" our hearts fluttered that such an exotic creature could be captured by such a homey term. Our fathers were not seen in zoos or museums once their children reached puberty. They did not meet in bars, but at their clubs. They did not loiter in public places waiting for people. When you saw them they gave your shoulder a squeeze or thumped you on the back in greeting. Our fathers did not look as if they had just woken from some drugged, sexual sleep. Their eyes did not have the glittering, mysterious light that made the heart of a teenage girl flop like a freshly caught fish.

. . .

Our social life was arranged for us. It included hot chocolate after skating, going to the movies in groups, studying
together for exams, and inviting friends for dinner—friends
who of course invited you back. When Delia came for dinner
we were embarrassed by everything: by the big, uninspired
American rib roasts and baked potatoes, by the insipid grape-
fruit and watercress salad, by the fact that a colored lady
(whom we called by her first name) served us, and by our
boring fathers and mothers trying to figure out what to say
to a child whose parents they had not known forever, especially this child whose father was a roué, whose mother
worked, and whose responses were the soft, correct, hidden
responses of a European child, not the loud, forthright man-
ners they knew.

When we were invited to the Schwanteses our mothers said
things like: "Oh, dear, don't you think it will be an awful
chore for Mrs. Schwantes to feed you after working all day?"

You changed your clothes before you went to Delia's for
dinner. We had servants but they had formality. You stopped
at the florist's and charged (at your mother's instruction) half
a dozen sweetheart roses to your parents' account.

The meals you were served by the Schwanteses were wonderful—nothing like the tame lamb chops and crown roasts
we were used to. Out of a glazed brown crock Mrs. Schwantes
served some fragrant stew made with wine. Even the potatoes
in that house tasted different—more of earth than of starch.
The salad had a dressing we thought of as grown-up, not like
the sweet boiled dressing we had at home. For dessert there
was fruit and cheese. We never rememberd the name of the
cheese, but if Mrs. Schwantes wrote it down for us and we
asked our mothers to buy it, it never tasted the same in our

dining rooms. We were given watered wine to go with the meal and after were served coffee in demitasse.

Every now and then Delia's much older sister Vanessa would appear. She was certainly the most beautiful girl any of us had ever seen. She had lived in Paris and now worked for a French designer in New York. She chain-smoked like her father and spoke rapid-fire French to her mother. Her shiny reddish hair was worn in a mop of curls, and her clothes were a more dashing edition of what her mother wore. Our sisters were by comparison very boring. Vanessa's life, we thought, was like one of those Japanese paper flowers that expands into a beautiful shape when put into water.

Vanessa made a point of ignoring her father. This piqued him—even we could see that. He hated that a beautiful woman—even his own daughter—did not pay any special attention to him or let him pay special attention to her. She poured him a glass of wine without looking at him. "Thank you, my darling," he crooned. How could she have resisted him? He spoke to her but she did not speak to him. All her remarks were directed to her mother, and her silence in his direction was full of contempt. In Vanessa's presence, he crumbled a bit. His eyes got a little dull, like a prize cat just beginning to get sick. Puzzlement about women was something he was not used to contending with, even in small doses. It wore him out. Delia and her mother simply behaved around the situation, and a less fanatic Schwantes watcher than I might never have known that Vanessa addressed not one word to her father.

This would never have happened in our households. If our sisters had frozen out our fathers they would have been taken aside by our mothers and given a lecture on not misbehaving in front of guests. Our sisters came home from college with politics and fought with our fathers because our fathers were rich, or if they brought home an odd friend they complained that our fathers were snobbish, or if they were entertaining some new idea, they were furious because our fathers were boring. But everything was out in the open. Doors were slammed. Meetings were held in various rooms. Threats were leveled. This was the American way. American children were expected to be rebellious: it was healthy and it didn't last very long.

After one of those dinners at the Schwanteses our parents seemed as sturdy and well designed as hotel china. Generations of American air, money, food and water, the milk of Holstein cows, and the democratic process had made them strong and forthright, with a steadfast, childlike belief in the security and correctness of their lives. But the Schwanteses had been fed on something subtler, less secure and more rarefied. They were delicate. They had depth and patina like nineteenth-century pottery. Their apartment had a dark, murky golden light which suited them. Everything about them was special.

We felt that Delia and her mother must have had some special bond. Often, they walked to school together. The sight of them was very poignant to us. We were truly separated from our mothers. Our school lives had nothing to do with them and what they did all day was of no interest to us. When our fathers left for work in the morning it was as if they had disappeared into thin air. Adult life, in our lives, was symbolized by a man and a woman dressing (she in the dressing room, he pulling his clothes out of the cedar cabinet and dressing in the bedroom and bathroom) to go out for dinner on a Saturday night. Adult life was jokes and references you did not understand, food (like iced coffee, martinis, and rare steak) that tasted awful to you, and ideas beyond your comprehension, like money.

In this milieu, the Schwanteses were our first taste of adult life. We saw the actual mother of a friend at work every day. We saw the friend's father, independent of the friend. We never ran into anyone else's father.

On the weekends, our fathers drove up to Westchester to play golf. Or they worked in their studies at home. But Mr. Schwantes, for whom the weekend was probably the best time for the sort of work he did, gave himself entirely to his family on the weekends. When the weather was fine they went on picnics—we were sometimes asked along—with a big wicker basket of sandwiches and bags of watercress, covered dishes of potato and sausage, and a spirit lamp to brew coffee on. They liked to drive to an historic place, or to see the leaves turn, or to some pretty or interesting town. On Sundays Mr. Schwantes walked Delia and her mother to the little Catholic church nearby and sat in a restaurant to have his breakfast. He himself never went to church. Then the family piled back into the car and they drove into the countryside for lunch.

The car was an old car with grey felt seat cushions, in which the Schwanteses took the sort of summer trips we thought only poor people took: car trips of America. We were sent to camp, or to France to live with a nice French family, or on a bicycle trip of the Lake District with Teens of All Nations. But the Schwanteses toured their adopted home. Mrs. Schwantes sat in the front tatting or doing crewel embroidery. Delia sat in the back with one of her French cousins: Lillian, Sylvie, or Marie-Luc.

The Schwanteses took seriously many of the things we took for granted. For example, music. It was part of female social life to attend the symphony. In the winter time we referred to these concerts as "the fur watch" as we saw our mothers and grandmothers and aunts and all their friends greet one another in sable, ranch mink, and seal. In the world's greatest music they seemed to find a form of relaxation: they liked a good performance of a conservative program—nothing they really had to listen to. Every once in a while a mutation in the form of a real music lover would spring up. I was one and Ellie Meyer was the other. Ellie's grandmother, in fact, had been allowed to study at the conservatory in Paris before she came dutifully back, married Ellie's grandfather, and set about producing Ellie's father. One night at a school function old Mrs. Meyer had met Delia's mother and father. From then on, she shared her tickets with them. She took Delia's mother to the opera and Delia's father to concerts. It was a pleasure to see him with Mrs. Meyer who was quite beautiful and formidable, with brilliant white hair. They were the first adult pair we had ever seen who were together for reasons having nothing to do with sex or family or money. They flirted and teased and conversed. When the topic of friendship was given to us for our tenth-grade essays, old Mrs. Meyer and Delia's father was what I pictured.

Most of us—Delia was the exception—lived rather casually out of one another's houses. We were comfortable wherever we went, since anywhere was just like home: the same silk curtains, good oil paintings in heavy gold frames, big pantries and good food, chinz sofas, colored cooks and walnut coffee tables, Persian rugs and big glass ashtrays. When things broke in our households, they broke with a loud crash.

We picked each other up and walked to school together, but to pick up Delia you had to make what almost amounted to an appointment, or she asked you.

The Schwanteses lived further over East than any of us, on a tree-lined street we found quite charming. Where we lived there were nothing but houses or apartment houses. But on the Schwanteses' block was a French hand laundry, a second-hand book shop, an antique dealer, and a dressmaker. The building they lived in was actually a converted tenement, with tile floors and painted tin ceilings. Unlike the rest of us who had extra rooms, the Schwantes apartment fit the family exactly: a living room, a dining room, a small kitchen, and two bedrooms. They had five different coffee pots, each of which brewed a different sort of coffee. In the kitchen was a pan for making crepes, a pan with an ornamental bottom for making some sort of waffle, and jars of dried herbs and petals for making tisanes.

Since they had no kitchen table, the Schwanteses took their breakfast in the dining room. That struck us as very elegant and old world. If you picked Delia up, you could see the remains of their meal—the two white bowls out of which Delia's parents drank their café au lait, Delia's juice glass and little coffee cup, the glass plate with the two rusks left on it, and a pot of jam. Our cluttered breakfast tables showed the remains of a big meal shared by an extended family—brothers and sisters, a guest, an aunt or a cousin. In the light of early morning you could see by their breakfast table that the Schwanteses had only each other.

We got our news about Delia's father from upperclassmen whose sisters, now in college or married, had (or had friends who had) spent afternoons with him. We learned that he took girls he met on buses or in museums for coffee at Hildegard's Tea Room, or the Petite Trianon. He met older women— Jane Dalsimer's mother was said to be one—for drinks at the Russian Bar or the Carlsbad Café. It made sense to us that he did things like that. Our fathers were not the stuff of romantic heroes—who would want to go to a café with one of them? But Delia's father was. You could not imagine him having anything as ordinary as a profession or a job. Spy was the closest we could get to a suitable occupation for him. We could see him smoking a cigarette and wearing a beret— standing at a train station, in the shadows. These images came from the novels we read and the foreign movies we went to see on Saturday afternoons. Our fathers had been in the war, but Delia's father had fought in the Resistance, which was quite another thing.

Our dealings with the opposite sex included infantile crushes on boys from one school or another whom we met at dances. When one of these boys liked you, he took any occasion he could to bump you. If you liked him back, your response was to slap him.

But to go for a drink, to sit in a banquette, to have a man light a cigarette, or light yours. The closeness of legs under the table. The whole thing seemed electrifying.

Mr. Schwantes liked girls like Mary Shiller or Grace Herbert, Vivvie's sister. These were the great beauties of our school, girls who were asked out to dinner by famous playwrights and bankers. He saw girls when they graduated from college, after their first marriages, their second babies, their divorces. He was fond not only of grown-up school girls but of rich women who lavished so much money and attention on themselves that they gleamed. He liked interesting- and ravaged-looking European women who wore beautiful, severe clothes—older women. He liked interesting-looking girls—some of them Vanessa's friends, no wonder she hated him—who wore trousers, smoked too much, and pouted. He liked big, windblown former debutantes who always looked nearsighted and skinny models with silvery blonde hair. When he was with his wife he looked subdued and solicitous, careful as he took her arm. He held her just close enough to make the hearts of his other conquests jump, should they ever run into him when he was with his wife. That closeness announced a bond understood only by the two of them, but the fact was that nobody understood anything about the Schwanteses.

For a long time I thought that my friends and I were all alike, even Delia, that perpetual foreigner. I thought we had identical hearts under our plaid uniforms, but I was wrong. I learned this just before my eighteenth birthday.

My classmates sat like good docile girls taking exams, but I could hardly sit still. I saw going away to college as an adventure. They saw it as one of the steps you take toward adulthood after which you settle down and get on with the business of life. I had never missed a school day except for sickness, but to give myself a taste of the freedom before me, I took a day off from school and spent it by myself. It was a warm, early spring day with that soft pale light that seems to be filtered through a haze of pollen and falls sweetly on your shoulders. It was a perfect day to wander aimlessly. I ambled in my favorite streets to see what they were like during the weekdays and had a happy, solitary lunch at the Lillian Candy Shop, a place that sold chocolates in the front and sandwiches in the back. It made me giddy to see, for once in my life, what a day would bring me instead of having it all nicely organized. What it eventually brought me was Delia's father.

By the time we met it was late afternoon, and the streets were gloomy in the blue light. A voice behind me said: "It is so difficult to recognize the friends of one's daughter when they are out of costume."

There he was. His lidded eyes glittered. His rich hair was combed straight back. He wore a turtleneck sweater, a camel's hair coat, and he was smoking a cigarette. It could be said that this was an accidental meeting but, in actual fact, this *was* his turf, the part of Manhattan that is filled with bookstores and cafés and spice shops. This was where Delia's father entertained—the Russian Bar was around the corner and the Petite Trianon was up the street. It would not be quite correct to say that I was looking for him, but I must have known that it was not all that difficult to run into him if I wanted to.

Nevertheless, the sight of him threw me into a panic. He was so physically near. I was so confused I did not even shake his hand. I felt that Delia's father could see right into me. He took my arm as if it were assumed that I was going to walk with him.

"It is clear that you have not been in school today," he said. "What have you been doing?"

I could hardly speak. I blurted: "What you do." By which I meant promenading. He threw back his head and laughed a deep, smooth laugh.

"I very much hope that you do not do what I do," he said. "You are a schoolgirl and I am a life waster. Now come and redeem my wasted day by taking the last part of my walk with me."

Every girl I knew would have said, without a moment's hesitation: "I'd love to take a walk, but I've got to get home. Nice to see you, Mr. Schwantes. Bye-bye." It would never have occurred to them to say anything else, and they would have meant it, too. But the idea of a walk with Delia's father thrilled me. I was exhilarated and terrified, and nothing in the world would have gotten me to say no.

He walked me to the river and down a flight of steps to the promenade. There was no one by the river. The sun had gone down, and the sky was just beginning to darken. My shoulders shook slightly, from the chill, I thought.

Delia's father lit another of his cigarettes, and the smoke from it made me almost dizzy. He had been talking, and I had paid no attention. I hardly heard him. I heard the sound of my footsteps and my loud heartbeat. When he finished smoking, he turned to me. His small, beaked features seemed to have been made only for seduction and observation.

For some people life divides undeniably into childhood and adulthood, and I knew I was one of them. Delia's father took my arm as if we had been dancing and simply spun me into him. I was rather tall, so we fit. His eyes glittered and he smiled. He moved me a step or two closer to the promenade wall, and there he kissed me as I knew he would. I kissed him back.

That Eros is depicted as a chubby baby with baby wings and little toy arrows, as we had learned in the History of Civilization, struck me as a terrible irony. To the virtually untouched girl I was, Eros reared up like a bobcat, clawing at its cage with great, strong claws and dangerous teeth.

Delia's father kissed me again. I kissed him back. The smell of that smoke, that cologne—of him—made my knees rattle.

Children are a tribe, and childhood is their tribal home. One false move and you lose everything. The tribe moves off without you. You forget your tribal language, and when you meet one of your former playmates they cannot understand or recognize you.

Somewhere Delia and my other friends were safe—setting the table, doing homework, watching the news, having a piano lesson—while I stood on the promenade, kissing Delia's father. Finally he let me go and looked at me without speaking. With his hand on my shoulder, he ushered me up the stairs to the street with the solicitousness you extend to people who have sprained an ankle or had minor surgery.

The streetlights were on. It was almost dark. The light was against us. My legs felt empty. If Delia's father had not been standing next to me, so close that our arms were pressed together, I thought I might have fallen in a heap. A few children were coming home from playing, and in that creepy darkness they looked jaunty and furtive, like animals who come out at night. The light changed. Delia's father took my arm. Those jaunty children skipped past us, and I crossed to my side of the street forever.

A Mythological Subject

It is often to the wary that the events in life are unexpected. Looser types—people who are not busy weighing and measuring every little thing—are used to accidents, coincidences, chance, things getting out of hand, things sneaking up on them. They are the happy children of life, to whom life happens for better or worse.

Those who believe in will, in meaning, in intentionality, who brood, reflect, and contemplate, who believe there are no accidents, who are born with clear vision or an introspective temperament or a relentless consciousness are quite another matter.

I am of the former category, a cheerful woman. The first man who asked me to marry him turned out to be the perfect mate. It may be that I happily settled for what came my way, but in fact my early marriage endured and prospered. As a couple we are even-tempered, easy to please, curious, fond of food and gossip. My husband Edward runs his family's import business. We have three children, all away at school. We are great socializers, and it is our chief entertainment to bring our interesting friends together.

Of our set, the dearest was my cousin Nellie Felix. I had known her as a child and was delighted when she came to New York to live and study. After all, few things are more pleasing than an attractive family member. She was full of high spirits and emotional idealism. What would become of her was one of our favorite topics of conversation.

In her twenties she had two dramatic love affairs. These love affairs surprised her: she did not think of herself as a romantic, but as someone seeking honor and communion in love. Her idealism in these matters was sweet and rather innocent. That a love affair could lead to nothing stumped her. When she was not seriously attached she was something of a loner, although she had a nice set of friends.

At the age of thirty Nellie fell in love with a lawyer named Joseph Porter. He was lovable, intelligent, and temperamental enough to make life interesting. With him Nellie found what she had been looking for, and they were married. Nellie believed in order, in tranquility, in her household as a safe haven, and she worked harder than even she knew to make sure she had these things. She taught three days a week at a women's college an hour outside New York. Her students adored her. She and Joseph expanded their circle, and eventually they had a child, an enchanting daughter named Jane. They lived in a town house and their life was attractive, well organized, comfortable, and looked rather effortless.

But Nellie did not feel that it was effortless. She had so ardently wanted the life she had, but she felt that she had come close to not having it; that her twenties had not been a quest for love but a romantic shambles; that there was some part of her that was not for order and organization but for chaos. She believed that the neat and tidy surfaces of things warded off misery and despair, that she had to constantly be vigilant with everything, especially herself. She once described to me a fountain she had seen on her honeymoon in the close of the Barcelona Cathedral. It was an ornamental fountain that shot up a constant jet of water. On top of this jet bobbled an egg. This seemed to Nellie a perfect metaphor to express the way she felt about her life. Without constant vigilance, self-scrutiny, accurate self-assessment, and a strong will, whatever kept the egg of her life aloft would disappear and the egg would shatter. She knew the unexamined life was not worth living. She never wanted to do things for the wrong reason, or for no reason or for reasons she did not understand. She wanted to be clear and unsentimental, to believe things that were true and not things that it consoled her to believe. When her colleague Dan Hamilton said to her: "You're very rough on me," she said: "I'm rougher on myself, I promise you."

My husband and I introduced Nellie to Dan Hamilton. We had been planning to get the Porters and the Hamiltons together for some time, but the Hamiltons were hard to pin down. Miranda Hamilton was a designer whose work frequently took her abroad. Dan was an historian. Once every three or four years he would produce a popular and successful book on some figure in colonial history. Over the years these books had made him rich, and he had become a sort of traveling scholar. Now that their three sons were grown-up and married they had more or less settled down in New York. Dan had taken a sabbatical from writing and was the star appointment at Nellie's college—all the more reason to bring the two couples together.

They got along famously. My husband and I looked down from our opposite ends of the table flushed with the vision of a successful dinner party. How attractive they all looked in the candlelight! Joseph, who was large, ruddy, and beautifully dressed, sat next to Miranda. They were talking about Paris. Miranda wore her reddish hair in a stylish knot. She was wiry and chic and smoked cigarettes in a little black holder. Nellie sat next to Dan. Her clothes, as always, were sober and she looked wonderful. She had straight ashy hair that she pulled back off her face and hazel eyes full of motion and expression. Dan, who sat next to her, was her opposite. As Nellie was immaculate and precise, Dan looked antic and boyish. He had a mop of curly brown, copper, and grey hair, and he always looked a little awry. His tie was never quite properly tied, and the pockets of his jackets sagged from carrying pipes and books and change in them. He and Nellie and my husband were being silly about some subject or other at their end of the table, and Nellie was laughing.

Over coffee it was discovered that Nellie and Dan shared the same schedule. Dan said: "In that case I ought to drive you up to school. I hate to drive alone and the trains are probably horrible." At this Miranda gave Dan a look which Nellie registered against her will. She imagined that Dan was famous for loving to drive alone and that he was teasing Miranda by flirting.

But the idea of being driven to school was quite heavenly. The trains *were* awful. The first week of Dan and Nellie's mobile colleagueship was a great success. They talked shop, compared notes on faculty and classes and family. Dan knew some of the people who had taught Nellie at college. The time, on these trips, flew by.

After two weeks Nellie became uneasy about the cost of gas and tolls and insisted on either paying for them or splitting them. Dan would not hear of this so Nellie suggested that she give him breakfast on school days to even up the score. Dan thought this was a fine idea. Nellie was a good plain cook. She gave Dan scones, toasted cheese, sour cream muffins, and coffee with hot milk. On Thursdays when they did not have to be at school until the afternoon they got into the habit of having lunch at Nellie's. They sat in the kitchen dining off the remains of last night's dinner party.

A million things slipped by them. Neither admitted how much they looked forward to their rides to school, or their breakfasts or their unnecessary Thursday lunches. Nellie told herself that this arrangement was primarily a convenience, albeit a friendly one.

One stormy autumn night, full of purple clouds and shaking branches, Nellie and Dan sat for longer than usual in front of Nellie's house. They were both restless, and Nellie's reluctance to get out of the car and go home disturbed her. Every time she got set to leave, Dan would say something to pull her back. Finally she knew she had to go, and on an unchecked impulse she reached for Dan's hand. On a similarly unchecked impulse, Dan took her hand and kissed it.

What happened was quite simple. Nellie came down with the flu—no wonder she had felt so restless. She canceled her classes and called Dan to tell him. He sounded rather cross, and it was clear he did not like to have his routines interrupted.

On Thursday she was all recovered, but Dan turned up in a terrible mood. He bolted his breakfast and was anxious to get on the road. Once they hit the highway he calmed down. They discovered that both Miranda and Joseph were away on business and that Jane was on an overnight school trip. They decided to stop for dinner at the inn they always passed to see if it was any good.

That day Nellie felt light and clear and full of frantic energy. She taught two of the best classes she had ever taught, but she was addled. She who never lost anything left her handbag in her office and her class notes in the dining commons. Although she and Dan usually met in the parking lot, they had arranged to meet in front of the science building, but both kept forgetting what the plan was, necessitating several rounds of telephone calls.

Finally they drove through the twilight to the inn. The windows were made of bull's-eye glass, and there were flowers on the sideboard. Nellie and Dan sat by the fireplace. Neither had much in the way of appetite. They talked a blue streak and split a bottle of wine.

Outside it was brilliantly clear. The sky was full of stars, and the frosty, crisp air smelled of apples and woodsmoke. Dan started the car. Then he turned it off. With his hands on the steering wheel he said: "I think I've fallen in love with you and if I'm not mistaken, you've fallen in love with me."

It is true that there is something—there is everything—undeniable about the truth. Even the worst true thing fills the consciousness with the light of its correctness. What Dan said was just plain true, and it filled Nellie with a wild surge of joy.

It explained everything: their giddiness, their unwillingness to part, those unnecessary lunches and elaborate breakfasts.

"My God," she said. "I didn't mean for this to happen." She knew in an instant how much care she had been taking all along—to fill her conversation with references to Joseph and Jane, to say "us" and not "me," not to say any flirtatious or provocative thing. How could she have not seen this coming? Falling in love is very often not flirtatious. It is often rather grave, and if the people falling in love are married the mention of a family is not so much a banner as it is a bullet-proof vest.

They sat in the cold darkness. Someone looking in the window might have thought they were discussing a terminal illness. Nellie stared at the floor. Dan was fixated on the dashboard. Neither said a word. They were terrified to look at one another—frightened of what might be visible on the other's face. But these things are irresistible, and they were drawn into each other's arms.

They drove home the long way through little towns and villages. Nellie sat close to Dan, who kept his arm around her and drove with one hand, like a teenage boy. At every stop sign and red light they kissed each other. Both of them were giddy and high. They talked and talked—like all lovers worth their salt they compared notes. They had dreamed and daydreamed about each other. They recited the history of their affections: how Dan had once come close to driving the car off the road because he was staring at Nellie one afternoon; how the sight of Dan with his shirttail out had brought Nellie near to tears she did not understand, and so on.

With their families away they had the freedom to do anything they liked but all they did was to stand in Nellie's kitchen and talk. They never sat down. When they were not talking they were in each other's arms, kissing in that way that is like drinking out of terrible thirst. Twice Nellie burst into tears—of confusion, desire, and the terrible excess of happiness that love and the knowledge that one is loved in return often brings. Nellie knew what she was feeling. That she was feeling it as a married woman upset her terribly, but the feeling was undeniable and she did not have the will to suppress it. They stood on opposite sides of the kitchen—this was Nellie's stage direction—and discussed whether or not they should go to bed. They were both quite sick with desire but what they were feeling was so powerful and seemed so dangerous that the idea of physical expression scared them to death.

Very late at night Nellie sent Dan home. In two separate beds in two separate places, in Nellie's house and Dan's apartment, separated by a number of streets and avenues, these two lovers tossed and ached and attempted to sleep away what little of the night remained to them.

The next morning Nellie woke up exhausted and keen in her empty house. When she splashed water on her face to wake herself up she found that she was laughing and crying at the same time. She felt flooded by emotions, one of which was gratitude. She felt that her life was being handed back to her, but by whom? And from where?

Alone in her kitchen she boiled water for tea and thought about Dan. For a moment he would evaporate and she could not remember what had passed between them. She drank her tea and watched a late autumn fly buzz around the kitchen. When it landed on the table, she observed it. The miraculous nature of this tiny beast, the fact that it could actually fly, the complexities and originality of things, the richness of the world, the amazing beauty of being alive struck Nellie full force. She was filled up, high as a kite. Love, even if it was doomed, gave you a renewed sense of things: it did hand life back to you.

But after a certain age, no joy is unmitigated. She knew that if she did not succeed in denying her feelings for Dan her happiness in his presence would always mix with sadness. She had never been in love with anyone unavailable, and she had never been unavailable herself.

Her heart, she felt, was not beating properly. She did not

think that she would take a normal breath until she heard from Dan. When the telephone rang, she knew it was him.

"May I come and have breakfast with you?" he said. "Or do you think it's all wrong."

Nellie said: "It's certainly all wrong but come anyway."

This was their first furtive meeting. Friday was not a school day: they were meeting out of pure volition. If Joseph asked her what she had been up to she could not say casually: "Dan Hamilton stopped by." It might sound as innocent as milk, but they were no longer innocent.

The sunlight through the kitchen windows suddenly looked threatening. The safe, tidy surfaces suddenly looked precarious and unstable. Her life, the life of a secure and faithful wife, had been done away in an instant, and even if she never saw Dan Hamilton again it was clear that something unalterable had happened to her. She could never again say that she had not been tempted. She felt alone in the middle of the universe, without husband or child, with only herself. Surely at the sight of Dan everything would fall into place and everything would be as it had been a day ago. She would see that Dan was her colleague and her friend, and that a declaration of love would not necessarily have to change everything.

But as soon as she saw him from the window she realized that a declaration does in fact change everything and that Dan was no longer just her colleague and friend. They could not keep out of each other's arms.

"I haven't felt this way since I was a teenager," said Dan. Nellie didn't say anything. She *had* felt this way since she was a teenager.

"It feels sort of heavenly," Dan said.

"It will get a little hellish," Nellie said.

"Really?" said Dan. "It's hard to believe."

"I've felt this way a couple of times," said Nellie. "Back in

the world of childhood when everyone was single and nothing
got in the way of a love affair. You could spend your every
minute with the one you loved. You could have the luxury of
getting *tired* of the one you loved. You had endless time. This
is the grown-up world of the furtive, adulterous love match.
No time, no luxury. I've never met anyone on the sly."

"We don't have to meet on the sly," said Dan. "We're
commuters."

"I don't think you realize how quickly these things get out
of hand," Nellie said.

"I'd certainly like to find out," said Dan, smiling. "Can't we
just enjoy our feelings for a few minutes before all this furtive
misery comes crashing down on us?"

"I give it an hour," said Nellie.

"Well, all right then. Let's go read the paper. Let's go into
the living room and cozy up on the couch like single people. I
can't believe you actually went out this morning and got the
paper. You must have it delivered."

"We do," said Nellie.

"We do, too," said Dan.

Miranda was due back the next day, and Joseph in the
early evening. Dan and Nellie stretched out on the couch in
the sunlight and attempted to browse through the paper. Physical nearness caused their hearts to race. Adulterous lovers,
without the errands and goals and plans that make marriage
so easy, are left horribly to themselves. They have nothing to
do but be—poor things.

"Here we are," said Nellie. "Representatives of two households, both of which get the *Times* delivered, curled up on a
couch like a pair of teenagers."

They did not kiss each other. They did not even hold
hands. The couch was big enough for both of them, with a
tiny space between. They kept that space between them.

Everything seemed very clear and serious. This was their last chance to deny that they were anything more than friends. Two gestures could be made: they would become lovers or they would not. It seemed to Nellie a very grave moment in her life. She was no longer a girl with strong opinions and ideals, but a mortal woman caught in the complexities of life itself. Both Nellie and Dan were silent. Once they were in each other's arms it was all over, they knew, but since falling in love outside of marriage is the ultimate and every other gesture is its shadow, when they could bear it no longer they went upstairs to Nellie's guest room and there became lovers in the real sense of the word.

Of all the terrible things in life, living with a divided heart is the most terrible for an honorable person. There were times when Nellie could scarcely believe that she was the person she knew. Her love for Dan seemed pure to her, but its context certainly did not. There was not one moment when she felt right or justified: she simply had her feelings and she learned that some true feelings make one wretched; that they interfere with life; that they cause great emotional and moral pain; and that there was nothing much she could do about them. Her love for Dan opened the world up in a terrible and serious way and caused her, with perfect and appropriate justification, to question everything: her marriage, her ethics, her sense of the world, herself.

Dan said: "Can't you leave yourself alone for five seconds? Can't you just go with life a little?"

Nellie said: "Don't you want this to have anything to do with your life? Do you think we fell in love for no reason whatsoever? Don't you want to know what this means?"

"I can't think that way about these things," Dan said. "I want to enjoy them."

Nellie said: "I have to know everything. I think it's immoral not to."

That was when Dan had said: "You're very rough on me."

Any city is full of adulterers. They hide out in corners of restaurants. They know the location of all necessary pay telephones. They go to places their friends never go to. From time to time they become emboldened and are spotted by a sympathetic acquaintance who has troubles of his or her own and never says a word to anyone.

There are plain philanderers, adventurers, and people seeking revenge on a spouse. There are those who have absolutely no idea what they are doing or why, who believe that events have simply carried them away. And there are those to whom love comes, unexpected and not very welcome, a sort of terrible fact of life like fire or flood. Neither Nellie nor Dan had expected to fall in love. They were innocents at it.

There were things they were not prepared for. The first time Nellie called Dan from a pay 'phone made her feel quite awful—Joseph was home with a cold and Nellie wanted to call Dan before he called her. That call made her think of all the second-rate and nasty elements that love outside marriage entails.

The sight of Nellie on the street with Jane upset Dan. He saw them from afar and was glad he was too far off to be seen. That little replica of Nellie stunned him. He realized that he had never seen Jane before: that was how distant he and Nellie were from the true centers of each other's lives. He was jealous of Jane, he realized. Jealous of a small daughter because of such exclusive intimacy.

When Nellie ran into Dan with his middle son Ewan at the

liquor store one Saturday afternoon, it had the same effect on her. Both she and Dan were buying wine for dinner parties. Both knew exactly what the other was serving and to whom. This made Nellie think of the thousands of things they did not know and would never know: that family glaze of common references, jokes, events, calamities—that sense of a family being like a kitchen midden: layer upon layer of the things daily life is made of. The edifice that lovers build is by comparison delicate and one-dimensional. The sight of the beloved's child is only a living demonstration that the one you love has a long and complicated history that has nothing to do with you.

They suffered everything. When they were together they suffered from guilt and when apart from longing. The joys that lovers experience are extreme joys, paid for by the sacrifice of everything comfortable. Moments of unfettered happiness are few, and they mostly come when one or the other is too exhausted to think. One morning Nellie fell asleep in the car. She woke up with the weak winter light warming her. For an instant she was simply happy—happy to be herself, to be with Dan, to be alive. It was a very brief moment, pure and sweet as cream. As soon as she woke up it vanished. Nothing was simple at all. Her heart felt heavy as a weight. Nothing was clear or reasonable or unencumbered. There was no straight explanation for anything.

Since I saw remarkably little of Nellie, I suspected something was up with her: she was one of those people who hide out when they are in trouble. I knew that if she needed to talk she would come to see me and eventually she did just that.

It is part of the nature of the secret that it needs to be shared. Without confession it is incomplete. When what she was feeling was too much for her, Nellie chose me as her confidante. I was the logical choice: I was family, I had known Nellie all her life, and I had known Dan for a long time, too.

She appeared early one Friday in the middle of a winter storm. She was expected anyway—she and I were going to pick up Jane later in the afternoon and then my husband and I, Nellie, Joseph, and Jane were going out for dinner.

She came in looking flushed and fine, with diamonds of sleet in her hair. She was wearing a grey skirt, and a sweater which in some lights was lilac and in some the color of a pigeon's wing. She shook out her hair, and when we were finally settled in the living room with our cups of tea I could see that she was very upset.

"You look very stirred up," I said.

"I am stirred up," said Nellie. "I need to talk to you." She stared down into her tea and it was clear that she was composing herself to keep from crying.

Finally she said: "I'm in love with Dan Hamilton."

I said: "Is he in love with you?"

"Yes," said Nellie.

I was not surprised at all, and that I was not surprised upset her. She began to cry, which made her look all the more charming. She was one of those lucky people who are not ruined by tears.

"I'm so distressed," she said. "I almost feel embarrassed to be as upset as I am."

"You're not exempt from distress," I said. "You're also not exempt from falling in love."

"I wanted to be," she said fiercely. "I thought that if I put my will behind it, if I was straight with myself I wouldn't make these mistakes."

"Falling in love is not a mistake."

She then poured forth. There were no accidents, she knew. That she had fallen in love meant something. What did it say about herself and Joseph? All the familiar emotional props of girlhood—will, resolve, a belief in a straight path— were gone from her. She did not see why love had come to her unless she had secretly—a secret from herself, she meant— been looking for it. And on and on. That she was someone who drew love—some people do, and they need not be especially lovable or physically beautiful, as Nellie believed—was not enough of an explanation for her. That something had simply happened was not an idea she could entertain. She did not believe that things simply happened.

She talked until her voice grew strained. She had not spared herself a thing. She said, finally: "I wanted to be like you—steady and faithful. I thought my romantic days were over. I thought I was grown-up. I wanted for me and Joseph to have what you and Edward have—a good and uncomplicated marriage."

It is never easy to give up the pleasant and flattering image other people have of one's own life. Had Nellie's distress not been so intense, I would not have felt compelled to make a confession of my own. But I felt rather more brave in the face of my fierce cousin: I was glad she was suffering, in fact. I knew she divided the world into the cheerful slobs like me and the emotional moralists like herself. A serious love affair, I thought, might take some of those sharp edges off.

I began by telling her how the rigorousness with which she went after what she called the moral universe did not allow anyone very much latitude, but none the less, I was about to tell her something that might put her suffering into some context.

"I have been in love several times during my marriage," I said. "And I have had several love affairs."

The look on her face, I was happy to see, was one of pure relief.

"But I thought you and Edward were so happy," she said.

"We are," I said. "But I'm only human and I am not looking for perfection. Romance makes me cheerful. There have been times in my life when I simply needed to be loved by someone else and I was lucky enough to find someone who loved me. And look at me! I'm not beautiful and I'm not so lovable, but I'm interested in love and so it comes to find me. There are times when Edward simply hasn't been there for me—it happens in every marriage. They say that it takes two and sometimes three to make a marriage work and they're right. But this has nothing to do with you because I picked my partners in crime for their discretion and their very clear sense that nothing would get out of hand. I had my bad moments, but nothing ever did get out of hand. I can see that an affair that doesn't threaten your marriage is not your idea of an affair, but there you are."

This made Nellie silent for a long time. She looked exhausted and tearstained.

"One of the good things about this love affair," she said, "is that it's shot my high horse right out from under me. It's a real kindness for you to tell me what you've just told me."

"We're all serious in our own ways," I said. "Now I think you need a nap. You look absolutely wiped out. I'll go call Eddie and tell him to meet Joseph and then when you wake up we can plot where we're going to take Jane for dinner."

I gave her two needlepoint pillows for her head, covered her with a quilt, and went to call my husband. When I got back I sat and watched my cousin sleeping. The sleety, yellowish light played over her brow and cheekbones.

She was lying on her side with her hand slightly arched and bent. Her hair had been gathered at her neck but a few strands had escaped. She looked like the slain nymph Procris in the Piero di Cosimo painting *A Mythological Subject* which depicts poor Procris who has been accidentally killed by her husband Cephalus. Cephalus is a hunter who has a spear that never misses its mark. One day he hears a noise in the forest, and thinking that it is a wild beast, he takes aim. But it is not a beast. It is Procris. In the painting a tiny jet of blood sprays from her throat. At her feet is her mournful dog, Lelaps, and at her head is a satyr, wearing the look of a heartbroken boy. That picture is full of the misery and loneliness romantic people suffer in love.

The lovely thing about marriage is that life ambles on—as if life were some meandering path lined with sturdy plane trees. A love affair is like a shot arrow. It gives life an intense direction, if only for an instant. The laws of love affairs would operate for Nellie and Dan: they would either run off together, or they would part, or they would find some way to salvage a friendship out of their love affair. If you live long enough and if you are placid and easygoing, people tell you everything. Almost everyone I know has confessed a love affair of some sort or another to me.

But I had never discussed my amours with anyone. Would Nellie think that my affairs had been inconsequential? Certainly I had never let myself get into such a swivet over a man, but I had made very sure to pick only those with very secure marriages and a sense of fun. Each union had been the result of one of the inevitable low moments that marriages contain, and each parting, when the right time came to part, had been relatively painless. The fact was, I was not interested in love in the way Nellie was. She was interested in ultimates. I remembered her fifteen years ago, at twenty-three, rejecting all the nice, suitable young men who wanted to take her out for dinner and in whom she had no interest. She felt this sort of socializing was all wrong. When my husband and I chided her, she said with great passion: "I don't want a social life. I want love, or nothing."

Well, she had gotten what she wanted. There she lay, wiped out, fast asleep, looking wild, peaceful, and troubled all at the same time. She had no dog to guard her, no satyr to mourn her, and no bed of wild flowers beneath her like the nymph in the painting.

What a pleasant circumstance to sit in a warm, comfortable room on an icy winter's day and contemplate someone you love whose life has always been of the greatest interest to you. Procris in the painting is half naked, but Nellie looked just as vulnerable.

It would be exceedingly interesting to see what happened to her, but then she had always been a pleasure to watch.

Saint Anthony of the Desert

Haphazardness, as a condition of life, has its usefulness but is of fixed duration. At the time of which I am writing, my life was entirely the product of haphazardness, and I had encountered no reason not to enjoy it. Along with being haphazard, I was lucky. These conditions are often found together, like gold and pyrite. For example, I was very bad about money. It flew out of my pocket, and I could not account for it at the end of the week. My checkbook was described to me as looking more like a poem in free verse than a record of my finances. Naturally, my checks, through no malicious intent of mine, were frequently sent back marked "insufficient funds." But unlike others who receive letters from their banks that begin: "Due to the sloppy and inconsequential manner in which you keep your account, we no longer wish to do business with you," I was telephoned by a harried bank flack named Dan Pirotta, who said, "Miss Greenway, if you will come over here some afternoon, I will be happy to show you how to balance your checkbook."

I also had a habit of losing my wallet. I left it on counters
and in taxis, and it was always returned to me, often with the
money untouched. My education was as hapless as my finances. As I had conducted it, it suited me for nothing. I had
been a cheerful student with a short but intense attention
span, waiting for some subject to commit itself to me. Since
none did, I floated from course to course and ended up un-
hirable. No one seemed to have a job for someone whose
qualifications included a love of American poetry, an imperfect understanding of astronomy, and a fascination with but
by no means a firm grasp of the principles of cultural an-
thropology. The job I got when I left school was in the gift
shop of a museum, selling postcards, calendars, and replicas.

After two years of this work and after my lecture from Mr.
Pirotta at the bank, I managed to save enough money to go to
Paris. Saving that sum of money was the most serious gesture
I had made in my life up to that point.

Once there, I threw myself on the mercy of my cousin
Charles, a much older relative who was an architect working
for UNESCO. I had chosen Paris for no discernible reason
except that one of my few skills was an ability to show off in
imperfect French. Charles had once been my baby-sitter. I
had not seen him in many years, but he took one look at me
and pegged me for one of those American girls who come to
Paris looking for adventure. It was clear that something had
to be done with me, so Charles sent me on a walking tour of
churches and cathedrals. Perhaps he thought that if I got inside those buildings I might acquire a little sense. He made me
check in with him every afternoon so that he could be sure
that I had not gotten lost or otherwise gone astray. To his
amazement and relief, I was enthralled. Here, I felt, was a
subject I might have a lifelong involvement with. I bought a
notebook and took detailed notes on what I was looking at.

. . .

As a reward for not being as hopeless as I appeared, Charles took me on a car trip to the Benedictine abbey of Saint Wandrille de Fontenelle. Unlike the ruined abbeys we had stopped to look at on the way, this one had real monks living in it. From the public side of the chapel I could hear them singing vespers. The fact that actual people lived in this building filled me with wonder. What sort of lives did they lead? Who had built this place? And were there principles on which religious buildings were planned?

On the way back to Paris, I pestered Charles with questions. What was the difference between a cathedral and a church? An abbey and a priory? Charles then asked me for my impressions and listened patiently while I rambled incoherently. From time to time, it would occur to me that I wasn't making very much sense and then I would shut up.

"Go on," said Charles. "This is very interesting."

Then I revealed that I had a notebook full of notes. My cousin said, "You seem to have some genuine feeling for form and space. Why don't you do something with it? You say your life has no direction. Why don't you go to architecture school?"

I explained that I could hardly do math, that I could hardly sit still, that I was sick of school and that I did not want to be an architect. After all, was he building cathedrals, priories, abbeys? Besides, I was not at all sure that I had any genuine feelings about form and space. I was not even sure how interested I was. I simply loved being in those buildings—that feeling of chill and reverence, the gorgeousness of that tribute to something higher. Listening to those unseen monks chanting plainsong had stirred me up. For I myself was overheated, had nothing to revere, had never deprived myself of anything.

There was nothing serious in my life, and I was so silly that my own face in the mirror hardly mattered.

Charles did not understand interest that did not translate into practical action, but he gave me the name of a friend of his who owned a bookshop. This man was Pete Ethridge, and the shop was called The Architect and Travel Book Supply. I was to go and see him for advice—what books to read, what lectures to hear, what trips, if I had any money, to take. In this way Charles set me on my path, for, if you behave like something with as little weight as a piece of paper, life may float you in the general direction of your inclinations without your having to figure out what your inclinations are.

When I got back to New York, I went to see Pete Ethridge and he gave me a job. His assistant had quit the day before, and although I had little to recommend me besides my cousin's name, I knew how to handle a cash register and Pete needed immediate help. Pete had been trained as a draftsman and he loved to travel. He dealt in new, used, and rare books —anything an architect or traveler might need. On one long shelf were Pete's favorite books—accounts of architectural travel such as *The Old Road, A Time To Be Silent*, and *The Towers of Trebizond*. In time I learned to stock, shelve, order, talk to salesmen, and do the bookkeeping. In general, I began to learn how to run a bookshop, and as I became more useful Pete took me along with him when he went to buy private libraries.

Under his minimal direction, I began to read. The unifying topic of this reading was religious architecture, but if one can be said to pursue this subject in a voluptuous way, I did. I read haphazardly but steadily for two years. I had nothing else to do, except work. I lived in a cheap, fairly pleasant apartment and conducted my social life with rowdy, fun-loving friends, all of whom had minimal jobs: they were actresses who worked as waitresses, poets who were readers at publishing companies, and students who were fooling around with their dissertation topics. I had had crushes, a few inconsequential romances, but I had never been in love. From time to time, a nice steady young man would fall in love with me: a resident at Bellevue Hospital; a lawyer I met at a lecture on baroque cathedrals; a young architect who hung around the shop for weeks on the pretext of seeing if a book he had ordered had arrived. But I did not want one of these nice young men. Their lives looked too plotted for me. I could not see myself safe and married, setting a dinner table with wedding silver and wedding plates and producing an ambitious, correct, and not entirely successful dinner for my in-laws.

I was happy the way I was. At night, if I came home early, I made myself weird dinners of eggplant. I liked working in the shop, which smelled of Pete's cigars. I liked what I was reading. Except for work, I had no schedule. It was impossible to say when I would be home. I thought it was a wonderful idea to go to Chinatown at four o'clock in the morning if someone suggested it. I thought seeing three movies in one day was a normal thing to do. If five people collected in one apartment, that was a party. One evening two boys came to pick me up at the same time, but that turned out well enough. We went to the movies and out for a drink, and it turned out that they had a college friend in common.

Why in the middle of this cheerful chaos I had elected to read about monastic and church architecture was not clear to me. I was not religious, not an architect, and not a medievalist. Pete, who had made a study of the native structures of Tibet and Lapland without visiting either country, thought it a perfectly reasonable pursuit. I felt that this subject had the appeal of the substantial, the enduring, the traditional—three things notably lacking in my life. The idea of permanence, of a fixed course of life, of belief, was consoling to me. Often I wondered whether I continued this research because it had been handed to me by my cousin Charles. People who are lucky are often superstitious. My superstition was the sort that throws in its lot with the talismanic. This interest was my good-luck charm.

One cold, rainy day, a customer whose name I can no longer remember gave me an inspired tip. It was a slow day, and I was sitting at Pete's desk reading Cardinal Gasquet's *English Monastic Life* and smoking a cigarette. The customer noticed my book. A conversation ensued, during which he asked me if I had read any of the lives of the saints. I said I had read *The Rule of Saint Benedict*, but that was about it. The customer suggested that I might find Saint Anthony interesting, since he is considered to be one of the founders of monastic life.

About a month later I found a monograph about this saint at a secondhand store. It had been written by a German theologian and was mine for fifty cents. I took it home and put it on my desk with all of the other books I intended to read.

I read it in a fit of restlessness one cold Saturday afternoon. I had been invited for dinner that evening by some friends of my cousin Charles, a couple named Karen and Philip Bridges. The Bridgeses were my good angels, in a sense. They liked to feed me, and they felt that I should have some glimpse of what a happy, orderly domestic life looked like. In order to be as impeccable as possible, I usually spent the afternoon before one of their dinner parties selecting my clothes, washing my hair, and lying in a bath preparing my story: I would lie back and rehearse my explanation of why Pete had not taken me to a bookseller's convention, why my job had not expanded, and why I had not yet approached Pete about making me a junior partner. Such things interested the Bridgeses. But since it was early and I did not yet have to begin this process, I picked up the monograph and began to read.

The story of Saint Anthony is well known, although it was not well known to me. As a young man, this rich Egyptian heard the Gospel and took it seriously. After settling the future of his sister, he gave away all his money and repaired to a cave. There he intended to live a life of solitude devoted to prayer. Instead, the devils we have seen in famous European paintings beset him. They came in all shapes and forms. There was no torment or temptation that did not flash before his eyes. At the age of thirty-five, he plunged into the desert to begin another form of hermitage. There he planted a garden, which was trampled on by wild beasts. The bread he ate was of the vilest sort. His holiness and wisdom attracted disciples whom he banded into a primitive kind of monastic life, and he died, full of serenity, at a very great age.

I was surprised to find how moved I was by this account. I liked what I saw as Saint Anthony's impetuousness—giving away everything at once. It made the youthful saint seem something of a hothead, the power of the Gospel notwithstanding. My image of the saint in his cave was that of a serious boy who in modern life might wear glasses and carry a slide rule. The idea of devils parading in front of that innocence made me feel protective. In fact, I hardly reacted to the saint as a saint at all, but as to some endearing person whose life was full of self-invented tests. I especially loved his scolding of the animals who trampled his desert garden. "Why do you do harm to me," the saint rebuked them, "when I harm none of you? Go away, and in the Lord's name, do not come near these things again." This scolding worked, we are told. I had thought that saints were enormous figures who performed heroic actions and miracles in the name of faith, but, aside from inadvertently creating a form of monastery life, Saint

Anthony had not accomplished very much at all in the world, except to *be* and to put himself in the way of things. And although I was hardly interested in sanctity, I was obviously interested in being and in putting myself in the way of things. Saint Anthony made me feel as if there might be some hope for someone like me, somehow.

These thoughts were dispelled as soon as I walked through the Bridgeses' door, which for me was the walking into another country. The Bridgeses represented all of adult life. They had substantial furniture and a silver service. At holiday time they gave parties, to which guests came in evening clothes. Both of them worked on Wall Street, and both cultivated their interests. Karen belonged to a group that read and discussed the works of famous philosophers. Philip was constantly upgrading his stereophonic equipment and buying subscriptions to the opera and the symphony. Both of them were interested in food. They went to wine tastings and belonged to a gourmet club. The meals they served were always correct and very good.

I was often invited to be a fourth at dinner, doubtless because I was younger and therefore less predictable. The Bridgeses liked to throw me in with their more conservative and stuffy friends to see what happened. Nothing very radical ever did, but the investment bankers were pleased to have a chance to explain the real world to a shiftless, undirected book clerk, and I had a chance to feel superior to a bunch of staid grown-ups who paid in rent each month more than I earned in half a year.

In ordinary times, devils are ordinary. You meet them not in caves but at dinner parties. The shape they assume is that of attractive mortals of the opposite sex. The Bridgeses had also invited an extremely attractive mortal by the name of Alden Robinson. I had heard him mentioned—he was an old friend of Philip's. There was a copy of each of his books on their shelf. Alden was a socio-economist. His books were published by a university press. These bore his full name: Alden C. W. Robinson. He had just given up his teaching post in California and come East to lend his fine mind to the World Economic Committee.

I assumed that Alden was one of the Bridgeses' distinguished stiffs—the sort of people who hardly existed for me, since I divided the world into adults and people like myself, the way a child does. The questions I asked myself, for example, about the boys I met were: Did they look as if they knew how to dance? As if they were any fun? Daring? Good kissers?

Alden was not a boy, but he had a nice grin, for a grown-up. His hair was shiny brown, and his eyes were blue. He did not look like he would be much of a dancer, and it was not yet clear if he was any fun, but he did look to be a good kisser. During cocktails, he conversed with the Bridgeses and stared at me. I paid attention to the attention, but not to him. During dinner, he focused on me entirely, and I was not surprised when much later he offered to drive me home. All adults had cars, and Alden had told an elaborate story at dinner about driving his across country. He drove me to my door, although I lived out of his way. I hesitated to ask him in for a drink. Was it too late for a respectable socio-economist? Would he think I was forward? It turned out that he asked me.

"Are you terribly tired?" he said.

"I'm not tired at all," I said.

"Then may I come up for a nightcap?"

I was too embarrassed to tell him that the only thing he might get as a nightcap was some awful old sherry someone had brought me a year ago, but when I gave it to him he did not seem displeased with it. While I made myself a cup of tea, Alden surveyed my apartment, which contained family cast-offs—furniture that was old and good, but all of it was broken or damaged in some way, and none of it matched. The cane seat of the rocking chair had two holes in it. The couch had a foot missing and it was propped up by a dictionary. It was clear that Alden noticed everything. I was alarmed at what he was thinking of the untidy pile of books next to the couch and the coffee cup and ashtray on the table. He paused in front of one of my few pictures—a framed plan of the London Charterhouse. Then he sat down. I drank my tea. He drank his sherry. Neither of us had a thing to say.

"It's nice just to sit here and look at you," he finally said.

This made me blush. "I don't understand anything about sociology or economics," I said. "That's why you're stuck looking at me."

"I find looking at you very interesting," said Alden. "Is there any chance I can come and look at you some more one day soon?"

Naturally he came back, and I fell in love with him. I felt that I was being pulled out of my old self and becoming a new creature. I felt that Alden was my passport into the adult world—a world in which things were planned and calculated. Since I was in love with him, the transition would be painless. I could not have asked for a better guide. Alden was established. His opinion was sought. He contributed to a number of journals. His own life was a miracle of precision. His desk was tidy, his bills were paid, he had regular checkups, and had his teeth cleaned every six months. In the autumn he had the chassis of his car painted with a rust-resistant paint. He had files for everything. But for all that he was not dull. He was nothing like those nice young men who had fallen in love with me. For one thing, he had been married and was now separated; he was not an untried boy. This made him seem glamorous. After all, no one I knew was married. No one I knew had any commitments whatsoever. And for another thing, Alden's energy was furious. His orderly life seemed to be the result of daring and risk.

My appearance in his life was a great relief to him, he said. I disturbed the neat universe he lived in—or so he claimed. I took life's suprises (by which Alden meant traffic jams, wrong turns, spilled drinks, delayed trains, and being spoken to on the street by insane people) in stride. I had no expectations, and so I was pleased and charmed with whatever fell my way. Alden thought we would be the perfect travel mates. He would make up the itinerary, he said, and I would get us lost. Thus we would see at least some of the things a traveler was meant to see, and then we would have adventures. Left to our own devices, I would never find a landmark, and nothing interesting would ever happen to Alden. We planned a trip to France for the next fall.

My availability for experience inspired him, he said. One evening, with a look of beautiful affection on his face, he told me: "The trouble with being prepared for everything the way I am is that one false move and you feel the world is falling apart. Last week, when I lost my keys, I thought I was going to disintegrate, remember? But you—you really *aren't* prepared for things, so you're much better at life than I am. If you hadn't been with me, I would have just gone to pieces. I would have paid a locksmith some huge sum of money. I would never have traced our trail back to that restaurant and found the keys under the chair. So maybe you're the one who's prepared and I am simply overprepared. You are a great object lesson to me."

How wonderful it was to have what I had thought of as an

unfortunate character trait looked at as a grace. I was often sick of myself losing keys and wallets. Of course, I was an expert at finding them. But Alden saw this as flexibility, esprit, lightness. Suddenly that lazy floating feeling I had always lived with was good for something, a virtue.

My function was to cheer him. I took him dancing. I bullied him out of tempers when the service was bad at restaurants. I saw us as teachers and students both. From Alden, I was learning how to give life some shape, how real work was performed in the world, how to harness energy to a project. I realized that I might be buoyant but I need not be untidy. I cleared my desk. I began to pay my bills on time. I bought a notebook and began to codify all the reading I had done and assemble all the notes I had taken. For a year Pete had been talking about redesigning the shop. He had asked me to sketch out any ideas I might have, but I had never taken him seriously. Now I did. I made elaborate plans, most of which Pete approved.

From me, Alden was learning how to float, how to relish life without such strict rules for it. Our best selves, I thought, were on display. The variance of our natures seemed like art—light and shadow. There were times I felt that I was Alden's pet, and that did not bother me a bit, since, in a sense, he was mine. He was a pet from another country whose life was not, like mine, a relief map full of valleys, hills, and moraines, but was a hard, straight road that got you to an appointed city. Alden was pleased with my relief map. It was full of turns he had never taken. I was entranced by his straight road. We had absolutely nothing in common.

Beneath his proper exterior, Alden was an eccentric. I felt that doting on these eccentricities was good for him—after all, wasn't it my job to make him giggle and swoon? I singled out his oddities and doted on them: that he could imitate a cat's purr; that he was secretly afraid of shaving and, since he hated electric razors, he distracted himself from the thought that he might somehow slit his own throat by walking around the living room while he shaved; that he hated to wear shoes. These things were what I thought personality was all about. I did not stop to think that to Alden they were frivolities. I thought that the world was an open proposition: if I got tidier and Alden got less fussy, we would go along beautifully forever.

One evening Alden sat me down and told me that it was necessary to have a serious talk. I had thought that *all* of our talks were serious, but I was wrong. I sat down on the sofa next to him.

"I think you'd better sit in the chair by the desk," Alden said.

I crossed the room and sat in the chair by the desk. Alden sat silently on the couch. Then he began to speak. He said his wife was coming to New York. What was she doing that for, I wondered. I had not paid very much attention to Alden's separation. When you were separated, that was it. Besides, Alden hadn't seemed to have given it much thought. It turned out that she was coming back to live with him—to try to work things out. What things? The very concept amazed me. If things didn't work out once, they never worked out twice.

Alden explained to me, in the sober way a doctor tells you what is wrong with you, knowing that he knows more than you do, that you cannot, without his training, possibly understand. He sits on his side of the desk—the side with the expertise on it—and makes you feel that you and your body are bad children.

"I am very grateful to you," was one of the things Alden

said. "You've helped me to free myself a little. But I work on the principle of commitment, and marriage is a very serious one. It is my obligation to do everything I can to honor it unless I find out that it is totally hopeless."

I did not say a word. Alden then went on to talk about his wife. Her name was Eleanor, and she was an economist, too. They shared a large store of communal memories. They had ideas and goals in common. Although the separation had been mutual, it had been Eleanor's idea to reconnect. That made immediate sense to Alden. Had it made immediate sense even while he was in my company? Those nights when I had watched him and he looked so dear to me, had it been his obligation to marriage he was thinking about?

It was not yet clear to me that Alden was packing me in and filing me under "an unserious romp with an entertaining girl." It was not clear that all the time we had played so happily together, Alden's real life, in what he thought was the real world, was lived apart from me. I thought for a moment that Alden had misread me—that he took high spirits for superficiality. I thought that perhaps he did not understand the gravity of my feelings for him, so I told him. These were the sacred words—the words I thought changed everything. Alden was now sitting on a rickety chair with one of the back slats missing. He repeated that he was very grateful to me, that our time together had been an enchantment.

I said: "But this is serious, Alden. I love you."

He said: "You'll get over it." And then he left.

I was not prepared for the aftermath of this affair. The distress I felt seemed uncontainable. At the shop I found myself in the bathroom in tears, running the faucets so that Pete would not hear me weeping. It was hard not to notice what bad shape I was in, so Pete asked me if I wanted the week off, but the thought of being alone with my distress horrified me.

What difference did it make that my bills were paid on time, that my desk was in order, that my research was actually taking some form, that the shop had been redesigned according to my plans, and that Pete was finally thinking of making me a partner? I did not look around to see that in fact my life was adding up to something after all. I only knew that my days were very long and my nights were unendurable.

I was beset by devils I had not known existed: grief, rage, longing, and pure desire. I fought back impulse after impulse to call Alden at work, at home. To confront him on the street. To track him down and make him see me.

After six months of this unrelenting misery, Alden reappeared. He rang my doorbell one night and came in. He wanted to see how I was doing. He assumed that I was doing splendidly since I was so buoyant, so spirited, so game. He was doing fairly well—the operative word was "fairly," he said. He and Eleanor were trying to work things out. A difficult business, but worth it. These gestures had to be made, and hard work generally paid off. This visit, Alden said, was purely casual—a doctor's checkup on the healthy. Alden snooped around my books, at my pictures, at my desk, just as he had the first night I had met him, except that he seemed entirely at home. His ease in my apartment broke my heart. I wanted to say, like Saint Anthony of the Desert: "Why do you do harm to me when I harm none of you? Go away, and in the Lord's name, do not come near these things again."

He did go away, and that was the last I ever saw of him.

On my street, people let their pets walk by themselves. I live on the shabby end of what used to be an elegant block of town houses. In front of one house sat a knock-kneed Irish setter who had been taught to flip the latch of the ornate iron gate with his nose. This dog walked himself up and down the street and then came back through the gate and spent the rest of the day sleeping on the stoop. A very stupid black and white kitten jumped from ground-floor window to parlor window, skittering away like a water spider if you came near it. This kitten, who belonged to a composer, had spent a night in almost every house on the block, taken in by suckers who thought it was a homeless animal.

There was also a fat white cat who could be found sitting by its owner's gate in the morning. Everyone stopped to pet it. If you stroked it, it would follow you halfway up the street and then walk back and wait for the next person to walk by.

The time of my most terrible sadness over Alden occurred during the winter, when the white cat stayed in. By the spring I felt that I was on the way to keeping myself together. The cat appeared on the street again.

One morning I stopped to pet it. I kneeled down next to it and scratched its ear. This cat was not discriminating. It was nothing I did but a whim of the cat's that made it jump into my arms and put its paws on either side of my neck. One can only fight sentimentality so long. The cat licked my cheek. I burst into tears.

For months I had been living in a cave with my own small demons. Now I was ready to go out into the desert, which was my life, through which I was bound to stumble. Unlike Saint Anthony, I had no militancy of faith to bring to bear against pain. A good bout with the devil does not leave you free of temptation and misery. My tears over that cat were simply tears of envy over what would never be mine to give again: that witless, spontaneous affection; that hungry, purposeless availability; that innocence.

The Smile Beneath the Smile

In the restaurant section of a local bar a man, a woman, and a small boy sat at a table having lunch. It was a cold January afternoon—the lazy part of the day when the lunch crowd had mostly left and the regular drinkers had not yet arrived. Two women, tired from shopping, dawdled over their hamburgers, their attention casually focused on the pretty family at the next table.

The man was in his early thirties, faunlike, boyish. The girl was in her middle twenties, curly-haired and lithe, with wide gray eyes. Both wore blue jeans and expensive sweaters. Between them sat the little boy, a towhaired child of exceptional beauty who was playing with a lump of clay.

The man was Andrew Dilks, and the boy was his son, Brownie, whose full name was William Brownwyn Dilks. The girl was Rachel Manheim, and she was well aware that they were being watched. It had happened before.

Yes, they were beautiful: Brownie in his own right; and

Andrew and Rachel, both attractive, had a glowing edge in their features. They had been lovers a year ago and had parted with a good deal of pain, but neither had been able to entirely give the other up. Although communication between them had ceased—Rachel was in New York and Andrew in Boston—they were as bound as if they had been together. The source of this bond was of little interest to Andrew. He felt it as a power and a pull—a pull toward Rachel and the power to affect her. Rachel, who had spent a year amazed that she could not get over Andrew, now realized that the bond they shared was one of awful sadness. Nothing good would ever happen to them again, no matter with what ardent innocence they approached each other.

They had met in the nicest way—introduced by mutual friends at a dinner party. On New Year's Eve they had fallen in love under the best circumstances: neither was interested in falling in love, so when it happened, they knew it was destiny. Andrew's life was crowded, so he felt, with obligations. He had been in the middle of his divorce from the former Carol Brownwyn. His responsibilites existed as he liked them to exist: neat, numerous, and plain as the nose on his face: Brownie, separation papers, the lawyers, his parents. Andrew conducted his life as if it were a decathlon. It kept him from feeling, or so his beloved Rachel had told him.

He and Rachel had parted shortly before his divorce became final. But with the divorce had come a new roster of problems: custody, grandparents, child support payments. When he was not attending to these unpleasant matters or was not engaged in his work—he taught pure math to advanced graduate students—it was Rachel who floated in front of his eyes. That he had hurt her didn't occur to him. He merely thought of her, of her hair, of her face in repose, the set of her shoulders, her laugh, the smile that lit her face. Late at night when he was half asleep, he composed wild, unfocused letters to her, letters which he forgot the next morning but which left him with the sense that he ought to *do* something about her. He had no idea what that might be.

Rachel's life was crowded, too, but not with obligations. She worked for a rare book firm and entertained a faithful set of friends. She enjoyed her work and had been making notes for a monograph on an Italian printer of the eighteenth century. Still, not a day went by—not a minute it seemed—that she did not think of Andrew. He hovered over her. He sat next to her on the bus. She heard his inflections in her own voice. She caught herself using phrases she had picked up from him.

This was their first meeting in a year, and time had not dimmed what they felt. They could not take their eyes off each other, but what was operating between them was longing and wariness. Their affair and its aftermath had marked them both. Each had been over it so often alone that the particulars —what he had promised or what she had said—were clouded by the event itself, and now they behaved as if something dire had *happened* to them unawares. Yes, they loved each other, but love in these situations is never enough. Rachel had written Andrew a terrible letter. He remembered the letter, but not what prompted it. Rachel remembered how he balked when after months of listening to his declarations of love, she had suggested they stop commuting and settle down together. He had simply turned on his heel, citing the complexities of his legal situation and his need for what he called a "clean legal image." And the questions Rachel asked about their future he treated like the idealistic statements children make about world peace. But what difference did it make?

The women at the next table continued to look at them, as who would not? When Rachel looked herself, she saw the source of her deepest love mired hopelessly in misunderstand-

ing, countercharges, and cross fires. Andrew simply saw
something he loved, would love, and that was the end of it.
Two more simple people would have either married or parted
and stayed that way, but such easily determined love does not
spring up between romantics; and Andrew and Rachel, had
they but known, were nothing if not hard-core romantics.
Romantic love takes its power from deprivation and innocence. It would be easy to subject it to the flat scrutiny of the
psychological, except that spirit is involved here, not pathology.

The women next to them were chatting and eavesdropping
at the same time. Shopping bags rested at their feet. As they
drank their Coca-Colas, they were witness to a moment of
beauty—the sight of that charged-up couple across the way.
They listened as Rachel talked to Brownie, whose stepmother
she once longed to be. Her attitude was loving, but cautious.
She was teaching him to make a figure out of his dirty, yellow
clay. Andrew said: "Remember, Brownie, when Mama gave
you that clay? She told you you could turn it into people."

Brownie said: "Mommy went skiing."

Andrew replied: "She'll be back soon."

At this, the women at the next table turned back to their
conversation. Some of the charm had gone out of the scene.
Why, that pretty girl wasn't the child's mother after all! Instead of an exceptional family, they realized that what they
had been watching was not so exceptional after all—a divorced man, his child, and some poor girl who got in the
middle of it.

If you live in a city, you cannot avoid inadvertently opening your life to strangers in public places. When you are in
love, happily or unhappily, you find eyes all over you. The
world is full of women—ordinary citizens, neighbors—
sipping Cokes and looking on with yearning, envy, pity, or
disapproval. If you turned your head to look at them, you

might wonder who they are, what they want, or what secret lovers haunt their pasts. But Andrew and Rachel, of course, didn't. For, although it reaches toward the Other, love is a self-involving pastime, and the fact of the matter is that no one else is ever as glamorous, as glowing. A love affair will teach anyone with sense a thing or two about aesthetics: love is artifice, like painting.

There were people in the world who found Andrew Dilks an ordinary-looking man. He had round eyes, a flat nose, and wavy hair. One of his front teeth was charmingly crooked, but so are the front teeth of a great many men who have been to good schools. When Andrew was with Rachel, he was not ordinary at all: he glowed. Rachel was a pretty girl by any standards, but in her state of love and longing and confusion, she was a positive vision. Although it is a cliché that beauty is in the eye of the beholder, most people feel that this useful phrase simply covers the vagaries of subjective taste. While this is true for paintings, with living beings in a highly charged emotional condition, the fact is that sheer faith in the beauty of the Other makes the Other beautiful. Andrew believed Rachel to be beautiful, and the power of his gaze—the gaze of the ultimate beholder—worked some change in her. A room full of people would have found her glorious under these conditions.

It is no accident that love finds expression in poetry. Love has nothing to do with personality. It has to do with form. Translate this into emotional terms, as Rachel was doing, and you find that romantic love has nothing to do with content, with commitment or weddings. It only has to do with love.

Love's homelier aspects are domestic. Consider Rachel and Andrew at Rachel's home. It was one o'clock in the afternoon. Andrew faced her in front of the fireplace. He had just rung the doorbell on the off chance of finding her in. This was no mere whim: he had been thinking of coming to see her when he had the chance and now he had. He and Brownie were in New York staying with Andrew's parents, since he had custody of his son during spring vacation, and it was easier to cope in the presence of a cook, cleaning woman, doorman, and two doting grandparents who were happy to take the flesh of their flesh to the zoo, or watch over him during his nap. Brownie was uptown, napping.

Above the fireplace was a mirror which reflected Andrew and Rachel's strained profiles. Their knees were shaking. Their palms were cold. The desire to embrace and say the hell with it, to kiss and wipe everything away, was rampant in both of them. Rachel could almost feel Andrew's soft lips on her brow. They were so close, they were almost touching. How easy it would have been to break the spell, and two less complicated people might have, especially with a lighter history behind them.

Rachel had already asked Andrew why he had appeared out of the blue. He had already said that he simply had to see her, and she had already wondered how much Brownie had to do with this: wasn't it nicer to spend your time with your child and your former lover than with only your child? She knew how much that question would wound Andrew and how close her supposition was to the truth. She knew as well, since this scene had been played over and over in their past and contributed a large part to their decline, that if she simply accepted the timbre in his voice and the stricken, passionate look on his face and gave in, several hours later he would tell her with much sadness that he had to leave. There was Brownie to look after, his clean legal image, his parents to answer to. She knew that as he stood there enraptured, he was calculating how much time he would allow himself to spend with her. What a sorry pass those faces in the mirror would come to.

Rachel said: "I wish you hadn't come. I want to see you, more than I can say, but I was in the business of biting the bullet and trying to get over you. Seeing you only sets me back, especially when I know you came here with nothing on your mind and that since you've got Brownie, you know in advance that you can't really see me at all."

During this speech, Andrew's face went through the fine tunings that had caused Rachel to love him from the first. The sweet smile of contentment—contentment in her presence—faded and was replaced with something pinched and exquisite at the same time. His eyes opened with pain and tenderness. Rachel flinched. That look was the beam of the headlights on the car that was about to run her over. He placed his arms on her shoulders and held his warm cheek next to hers.

"Oh, my God, Rachel, I love you so. I've always loved you. You're the angel that sits on my shoulder. At night when I'm working, I talk to you. You've become my thought process."

His tone was one of piercing sorrow. Rachel, who felt a sharp ache under her ribs, remembered that her moments of highest disappointment and loss had been accompanied by a terrible insight. It was true then. It was true now. The beautiful Andrew Dilks, who often watched her so closely when she talked that his lips moved with hers, did a brilliant imitation of a human being, except that the proportions were all wrong. His intensity was not born of excessive feeling, but of its lack. It was simply compensation.

But beauty sells the product every time, and Andrew Dilks had never come across so receptive a public as Rachel Manheim, so he sold her the only thing he had: a small need, easily fulfilled. If she cried, if she said she loved him, he would go away, not happy, but satisfied. But he would go away. *Go away!* After all that, Rachel could never quite believe that what he wanted was a quick hit of pure spirit, an emotional recharge that made him feel connected with the rest of his species.

Rachel spent her days working for the family Meyerhoff, four generations of rare bookmen. Three years engaged in this work was turning her into an expert, but at first it had amazed her that bibliophiles often like the binding better than the content. She had seen grown men spend vast sums on gold-embossed leather wrapped around an unreadable book. As she contemplated Andrew, who still held her in his sweet, tormented gaze, she realized she was perfect for her work. This beautiful binding stood before her, wrapped in his lavish emotions without any text. Andrew might love her, but he would not stay with her, would not marry her, would not arrange his life in order to let her into it, would not promise anything, except that he would carry his love for her throughout his life, wherever he was, which certainly wouldn't be around her. And what romantic lover can spurn a gift as rare as that?

Consider another conversation in a public place. Andrew and Rachel were sitting in a little café in Cambridge, Massachusetts. It was springtime and the fuzzy pastel buds were barely out on the trees. Rachel had come up for the weekend —it was her turn to commute. This commuting had been going on as long as they had known each other, and Rachel was beginning to tire of the strain it put on them. How nice it would be not to worry about train schedules or plane fares; not to be pressed for time. What she meant was, how nice it would be to feel normal.

Andrew was reading the paper. Suddenly, he put the paper down and looked at her. His grin turned into an expression of pure joy.

"Oh, it's you!" he said. "I never stop being amazed that you're here. When you aren't, I look up and expect you, but there's no one there. What a treat! I can actually reach over and take half of your croissant away."

This speech and its many variations served to make Rachel feel like a passing stranger.

"Well, then," she said, handing him the strawberry jam, "why can't we arrange it so that I'm here more? The Meyer-hoffs aren't the only rare book firm in the world."

"Then I could reach across the bed every morning and there you'd be," Andrew said.

"I don't think I'd have much trouble. I've been here on business a lot. I know the people I need to know."

"Then at night, when I start up my ritual conversation, I wouldn't have to conjure you up. You'd be here."

"I should call Fabian Mossman. I saw him a few months ago. He has a shop on Beacon Street."

"I'd have to lock you in the closet," said Andrew. "We'd have to have two different phones. Think of the work I'd never get done with you around."

"Oh, come off it, Andrew," Rachel said. "Don't make speeches about how much you miss me if, when I offer to move, you get balky."

At this point, the waitress brought the check. The conversation was forestalled and during a walk through the Busch-Reisinger Museum, it seemed inappropriate to bring it up.

That's romance for you. Only the necessary speaks, in the guise of the appropriate. And what is less appropriate to love, as Andrew Dilks had often pondered aloud to his adored Rachel, than the thought of lingerie and men's socks, drying over the same towel rack? People used to swoon at the suggestion of a kiss. Who swoons at the prospect of dishwashing and birth control? Love is ageless—it is about sixteen years old and lives around the time of Sir Thomas Wyatt. Poor Thomas Wyatt! Who else but a tortured lover writes a verse that begins: "They flee from me, that sometime did me seek," a poem that Rachel had recited to Andrew in the bathtub.

Great works of art are those in which everything fits perfectly, each part revealing the whole. Andrew and Rachel's love affair worked that way, too. Why else did Rachel read courtly love poems in the bathtub? Why did Andrew refer to Rachel's visit as a feast? Because the opposite was famine, and it was feast or famine with Andrew Dilks. Moderation was not within the spirit of the thing. Courtly love is, after all, a tradition of thwarted love. If Rachel wished to be cherished in this fashion, she would have to pay the price for it. Comfy, homey domestic life does not send you home on the shuttle inflamed. It does not cause huge telephone bills.

Rachel, since she had not been given the opportunity, wondered what it would be like to live with Andrew. Why, it would be wonderful, she thought, since she could not see beyond the pleasures of sheer availability. Of course, the mutual friends who introduced them had told Rachel some of the reasons why Andrew's marriage had broken up. That he insisted on turning off the heat in the winter and sleeping with the bedroom windows open, claiming that he had to cool out mightily in order to get to sleep. That when he stopped smoking and his wife reached for one of the three tasteless filters she liked to smoke in the evening, he flew into a rage and made her smoke in the cellar. That when she brought home a kitten that had lost its mother, Andrew threatened to drown it.

Rachel chalked that up to the unhappiness of a bad marriage. She knew that Andrew was a tease, and sometimes a cruel one, but she had never been the victim of direct abuse. Instead, Andrew nattered her to death. In New York, they slunk around like beaten dogs for fear of running into his parents' friends or Carol's. There was his legal image at stake, he explained. When Rachel reminded Andrew that Carol had left *him* and was only angry that the legal machinery was so slow in making their divorce final, he brought up Brownie. A fit father for Brownie would not be having an affair. When Rachel suggested that a fit father for Brownie might allow himself the happiness of a stable relationship, he lowered his voice and spoke unhappily of what might turn into a custody fight. That Carol was a perfectly fit mother and that Andrew did not want to be a full-time father was quite beside the point. All eventualities must be covered, Andrew felt. How easily these things get out of hand.

Rachel, an intelligent girl who favored the rational and orderly, could not believe that Andrew loved her as much as he said he did and not do anything about it. Her expectations were conventional, so of course she had forgotten how mutually exclusive this sort of intense emotional drama and a nice life are.

Be that as it may, she had allowed herself to sit at a table with what she most loved and could not have. She had gone with Andrew from her apartment to the Dilkses to pick up Brownie. The Dilkses were out, and the housekeeper handed the child over, still rubbing his eyes. Off they went, on a bus to a bar in Rachel's neighborhood to give Brownie his afternoon hamburger and glass of milk. Andrew said: "You remember Rachel, Brownie." Rachel remembered taking Brownie to the zoo, holding him up to see the monkeys, cutting up his peanut butter and jelly sandwich. She remembered Brownie, who loved her instantly, pulling on her coat. She remembered kissing the top of his white hair.

"No," croaked Brownie.

"Sure you do. She took you to the zoo lots of times. Remember?"

"Leave him alone," said Rachel. "There's no reason for him

to remember." Brownie was three then. He was now five. He didn't remember at all, but he responded to Rachel all the same. They sat watching Brownie pinch a little piece of clay into a shape that looked vaguely like a hat.

The truth had been learned and, if Rachel were not so ardent and Andrew so facially deceptive, the truth had been learned a thousand times. There is love and love. Why wasn't Rachel content knowing that Andrew would always adore her? He doubtless would. Taking care of love in the world— that is, nest building, homemaking, togetherness—is chicken feed in the face of this eternal feeling. If Rachel lived in a tower and Andrew were a gallant courtier, she would be perfectly happy to receive a caged nightingale from time to time, as a symbol, wouldn't she?

The women in their beaver coats were leaving. It was getting dark. They took a last look at the pretty threesome. Mournfulness had tinged the features of both Andrew and Rachel. Brownie was still absorbed in his clay—he had a long attention span for such a little boy. Rachel felt that she would scream if nothing was resolved. Then reason intruded. No, she would never marry Andrew and be Brownie's stepmother. She would not even have a satisfactory love affair. Andrew, if she agreed to see him again, would conduct their meetings like a series of two-car collisions. He would say he loved her and leave early. She looked at him and thought of what they had had. What *did* they have? Why, feeling. Pure spirit. A way of being that had nothing to do with ordinary life. All she was getting was an education in yearning, which was actually a four-point course in futility.

She looked at Andrew. He had gotten what he came for: an event, brilliantly emotional, so powerful that she could scarcely believe it wasn't real. If she let him, Andrew would continue to visit her in this way, leaving him satisfied and her bereft. Andrew sat in contemplation. His expression was one of poignant sadness. He was saying to her: "I love to watch your face move. You have that smile beneath the smile."

The women paid their bill. One of them came back to leave the tip. She stopped at the table—she couldn't help herself.

"What a lovely child that is," she said. The last beams of winter light streaked the table. It wasn't often you saw three people so beautiful, and so beautifully lit.

The Achieve of,
the Mastery of the Thing

Once upon a time, I was Professor Thorne Speizer's stoned wife, and what a time that was. My drug of choice was plain, old-fashioned marijuana—these were the early days when that was what an ordinary person could get. By the time drugs got more interesting, I felt too old to change. I stood four-square behind reefer except when a little opiated hash came along, which was not often.

Thorne was an assistant professor when I first met him. I took his Introduction to Modern European History—a class I was compelled to take and he was forced to teach. Thorne was twenty-seven and rather a young Turk. I was twenty-one and rather a young pothead. I sat in the back of the class and contemplated how I could get my hands on Thorne and freak him out. I liked the idea that I might bring a little mayhem into the life of a real adult. Thorne was older and had a job. That made him a real citizen in my eyes. He also had an extremely pleasing shape, a beautiful smile, and thick brown hair. His manner in class was absolutely professional and rather condescending. Both of these attitudes gave me the shivers.

I employed the tricks childish adolescents use to make the substitute math teacher in high school nervous. I stared at his fly. Then I stared at him in a wide-eyed, moronic way. At a point of desperation when I felt he would never notice me, I considered drooling. I smiled in what I hoped was a promising and tempting fashion.

It turned out that Thorne was not so hard to get. He was only waiting for me to stop being his student and then he pounced on me. I was high during our courtship so I did not actually notice when things got out of hand. I was looking for a little fun. Thorne wanted to get married. I felt, one lazy afternoon when a little high-quality grass had unexpectedly come my way, that a person without ambitions or goals should do something besides smoke marijuana, and marriage was certainly something to do. Furthermore, I was truly crazy about Thorne.

I got wrecked on my wedding day. I stood in front of the mirror in my wedding dress and stared intently at my stick of grass. You should not smoke this on this day of days, I said to myself, lighting up. Surely if you are going to take this serious step, I said, inhaling deeply, you ought to do it straight.

You may well imagine how hard it was for an innocent college girl to score in those dark times. You had to run into some pretty creepy types to get what you wanted. These types preferred heavier substances such as smack and goofballs. How very puzzled they were at the sight of a college girl in her loafers and loden coat. For a while they thought I was a narc. After they got used to me they urged me to stick out my arm and smack up with them, but I declined. The channels through which you found these types were so complicated that by the time you got to them you forgot exactly how you got to them in the first place, and after a while they died or disappeared or got busted and you were then left to some jerky college boy who sold speed at exam time as well as some sort of homegrown swill that gave you a little buzz and a headache.

Of course I did not tell Thorne that I used this mild but illegal hallucinogen. He would have been horrified, I believed. I liked believing that. It made me feel very free. Thorne would take care of the worrying and I would get high. I smoked when he was out of the room, or out of the house. I smoked in the car, in the bathroom, in the attic, in the woods. I thanked God that Thorne, like most privileged children, had allergies and for a good half of the year was incapable of detecting smoke in the house. And of course, he never noticed that I was stoned since I had been stoned constantly since the day we met.

Thorne took me away to a pastoral men's college where there were sure to be no drugs, I felt. That was an emblem of how far gone I was about him—that I could be dragged off to such an environment. However, a brief scan of the campus turned up a number of goofy stares, moronic giggles, and out-of-it grins. It did not take me long to locate my fellow head.

In those days professors were being encouraged to relate meaningfully to their students. I did my relating by telephone. Meaningful conversations took place, as follows:

"Hello, Kenny. Am I calling too early?"

"Wow, no, hey Mrs. Speizer."

"Say, Kenny. Can't you just call me Ann." I was only three years older than Kenny but being married to a faculty member automatically made one a different species.

"Hey," said Kenny. "I'll call you Mrs. Ann."

"Listen, Kenny. Is it possible to see you today on a matter of business?"

"Rightaway, Mrs. Ann. I'll meet you at six in front of the Shop-Up."

That's how it was done in those days. You met your connection in an inconspicuous place—like the supermarket, and he dropped a nickel bag—generally all these boys sold—on top of your groceries and you slipped him the money. Things were tough all right. Furthermore, the administrations of these colleges were obsessed by the notion that boys and girls might be sleeping together. Presumably the boys would have had to sleep with the drab girls from the girls' college ten miles away which had a strict curfew. Or they would be forced to hurl themselves at the campus wives who were of two varieties: ruddy, cheerful mothers of three with master's degrees, private incomes, foreign cars, and ten-year marriages. Then there were older wives with grey hair, grown sons, old mink coats, and station wagons. These women drank too much sherry at parties and became very, very still. Both kinds of wife played tennis, and their houses smelled evocatively of a substance my ultimate connection, Lionel Browning, would call "Wasp must." Both of these kinds of wives felt that students were animals; and they didn't like me very much either.

I was quite a sight. I was twenty-three and I wore little pink glasses. I wore blue jeans, polished boots, and men's shirts. For evening wear I wore extremely short skirts, anticipating the fashion by two or three years. I drove the car too fast, was not pregnant, and liked to listen to the Top 40. Faculty wives looked at me with fear—the fear that I knew something they did not know. When they had been my age they had already produced little Amanda or Jonathan and were about to start little Jeremy or Rachel. They wore what grown-up women wore, and they gave bridge and tea parties. These women lived a life in which drugs were what you gave your child in the form of orange-flavored aspirin so they did not, for example, go rooting around the campus looking for someone off of whom to score.

The older wives said to Thorne, whom they adored: "Gracious, Thorne, don't Ann's legs get cold in those little skirts? Goodness, Thorne, I saw Ann *racing* around in the car with the radio on *so* loud." These women hadn't seen anyone like me before, but years later after a few campus riots they would see a much more virulent and hostile form of me in large numbers. From my vantage point between the world of students and the world of faculty it was plain to see how much professors hated students who, since they had not yet passed through the heavy gates of adulthood, were considered feckless, stupid, with no right to anything.

It was assumed that Thorne was married to a hot ticket, but no one was sure what sort. This pleased Thorne—he did not mind having a flashy wife, and since I never misbehaved I caused him no pain, but I looked as if I were the sort to misbehave and this secretly pleased him. My image on campus however was not my overriding concern. I was mostly looking for decent grass.

Connecting on the college campus of the day was troublesome. Everyone was paranoid. I was lucky that I did not have to add money to my worries—I had a tiny bit of inheritance, just enough to keep me happy. I was a good customer when I could find a supplier, mostly some volelike and furtive-looking boy. Those blithe young things who spent their high school days blowing dope in suburban movie houses had not yet appeared on campus—how happy we would all be to see them! One's connection was apt to flunk out or drop out, and once in a while they would graduate. As a result, I was passed hand to hand by a number of unsavory boys. For example, the disgusting Steve, who whined and sniffled and sold very inferior dope. Eventually Steve was thrown out of school and I was taken over by another unpleasant boy by the name of Lester Katz. He carried for Lionel Browning, and Lionel Browning was the real thing.

Lionel, who allowed himself to be called Linnie by those close to him, had laid low for his first three years at college. In his senior year he expanded from a self-supplier to a purveyor of the finest grass to only the finest heads—by that time there were enough to make such a sideline profitable. Lionel's daddy was an executive in a large company that had branches abroad. Lionel had grown up in Colombia, Hong Kong, and Barbados, three places known for fine cannabis. He was a shadowy figure at college. He lived off campus and was not often seen except by my husband Thorne, whose favorite student he was. I had never seen him—he sent Lester to bring me my dope, with messages such as: "Mr. Browning hopes you will enjoy this sampling." It killed Lester that he called Lionel "Mr. Browning." He said it killed Lionel that Professor Speizer's wife was such a head. When he said that, I looked into his beady little eyes and it seemed a very good idea for me to go and check out this Lionel Browning who very well might have it in mind to blackmail me. Or maybe he was the uncool sort—the sort who might sidle up to his favorite professor and say: "That dope I laid on your wife sure is choice."

Lionel lived off campus in a frame house. Only very advanced students lived off campus. On campus rooms were very plush—suites with fireplaces and leaded glass windows. But the off campus fellows considered themselves above the ordinary muck of college life. These boys were either taking drugs or getting laid or were serious scholars who could not stand the sight of their fellow boy in such quantities.

Lionel lived on the top floor and as I mounted the stairs—I

had, of course, made an appointment—I expected that he would be a slightly superior edition of the runty, unattractive boys who sold dope. This was not the case at all. He looked, in fact, rather like me. He was blond, tall but small boned, and he wore blue jeans, loafers with tassels, a white shirt, and a blue sweater—almost the replica of what I was wearing. He smiled a nice, crooked smile, offered me a joint, and I knew at once that I had found what I was looking for.

Lionel did not fool around. He got bricks—big *Survey of English Literature*-size bricks of marijuana that came wrapped in black plastic and taped with black tape. Underneath this wrapping was a rectangular cake of moist, golden greenish brown grass—a beautiful sight. It was always a pleasure to help Linnie clean this attractive stuff. We spread newspapers on the floor and strained it through a coarse sieve. The dregs of this Linnie would sell to what he called the lower forms of life.

The lower forms included almost everyone on campus. The higher forms included people he liked. His own family, he said, was a species of mineral-like vegetation that grew on lunar soil. There were four children, all blond, each with a nickname: Leopold (Leafy), Lionel (Linnie), Mary Louise (Mally), and Barbara (Bumpy or Bumps). His family drove Linnie crazy, and the thought of their jolly family outings and jolly family traditions caused him to stay high as often as possible, which was pretty often.

In matters of dope, it depends on who gets to you first. I was gotten to in Paris, the summer before I went off to college. I looked up the nice sons of some friends of my parents, and they turned me on. I had been sent to practice French and to have a broadening cultural experience. I learned to

say, among other things: "Yes, this African kif is quite heavenly. Do you have more? How much more? How much will
you charge me per matchbox?"

The nice boys I looked up had just come back from Spain.
They were giant heads and they had giant quantities. These
boys were happy to get their mitts on such a receptive blank
slate as me. Pot, they told me, was one of the great aids to
mental entertainment. It produced unusual thoughts and brilliant insights. It freed the mind to be natural—the natural
mind being totally open to the hilarious absurdities of things.
It mixed the senses and gave flavor to music. All in all, well
worth getting into. We would get stoned and go to the movies
or listen to jazz or hang around talking for what may have
been minutes and may have been hours. This was more fun
than I ever imagined, so my shock when I went off to college
and discovered my fellow head was profound. My fellow head
was sullen, alienated, mute when high, inexpressive, and no
fun at all. Until I met Lionel, I smoked alone.

Lionel was my natural other. Stoned we were four eyes and
one mind. We were simply made to get high together—we felt
exactly the same way about dope. We liked to light up and
perambulate around the mental landscape seeing what we
could see. We often liked to glom onto the *Jill and Bill Show*
—that was what we called one of the campus's married couples,
Jill and Bill Benson. Jill and Bill lived off campus, baked their
own bread, made their own jam and candles, and knitted
sweaters for each other. Both of them were extremely rich and
were fond of giving parties at which dreadful homemade hors
d'oeuvres and cheap wine were served. Linnie and I made up
a Broadway musical for them to star in. It was called *Simple
on My Trust Fund.* We worked mostly on the opening scene.
Jill and Bill are in the kitchen of their horrid apartment. Jill is
knitting. Bill is stirring a pot of jam. A group of ordinary

students walks by the open window. "Jill and Bill," they say. "How is it that you two live such a groovy, cool, and close-to-the-earth life?"

Jill and Bill walk to center stage, holding hands. "Simple," each coos. "On my trust fund." And the chorus breaks into the lovely refrain. Once in the coffee shop Jill confessed to Linnie that she only had "a tiny little trust fund." This phrase was easily worked into the *Jill and Bill Show*.

Jill and Bill, however, appeared to be having something of a hard time. They were seen squabbling. Jill was seen in tears at the Shop-Up. They looked unhappy. Jill went off skiing by herself. I had very little patience with Jill and Bill. I felt that with all that money they ought to buy some machine-made sweaters and serve store-bought jam. Furthermore, I felt it was slumming of them to live in such a crummy apartment when the countryside was teeming with enchanting rural properties. The idea of a country house became a rallying cry—the answer to all of Jill and Bill's trouble.

Linnie mused on Jill and Bill. What could be their problem, he wondered, rolling a colossal joint.

"They're both small and dark," I said. Linnie lit up and passed the joint to me. I took a life-affirming hit. "Maybe at night they realize what they look like and in the morning they're too depressed to relate to each other. What do you think?"

"I think Jill and Bill are a form of matted plant fiber," said Linnie. "I think they get into bed and realize that more than any other single thing, they resemble that stuff those braided doormats are made of. This clearly has a debilitating effect on them. This must be what's wrong. What do you think, Mrs. Ann?"

"A country house," I said. "They must buy a lovely country house before it's too late."

That was the beginning of *Ask Mrs. Ann*, a routine in which Linnie and I would invent some horrible circumstance for Jill and Bill. Either of us could be Mrs. Ann. It didn't matter which. One of us would say, for instance: "Answer this one, Mrs. Ann. Jill and Bill have just had a baby. This baby is a Negro baby, which is odd since neither Jill nor Bill is Negro. Naturally, this causes a bit of confusion. They simply cannot fathom how it happened. At any rate, this baby has webbed feet and tiny flippers. Jill finds this attractive. Bill less so. Meanwhile Jill has bought a sheep and a loom. It is her girlish dream to spin wool from her own sheep, but the sheep has gone berserk and bitten Bill. In the ensuing melee the loom has collapsed, dislocating Jill's shoulder. Meanwhile, Bill, who has had to have forty stitches in his thigh as the result of violent sheep bite, has gone into the hospital for a simple tonsillectomy and finds to his amazement that his left arm has been amputated—he is left-handed as you recall. Jill feels they ought to sue, but to Bill's shock, he finds that he has signed a consent to an amputation. How can this have happened? He simply can't fathom it. But there is relief in all this, if only for Jill. Jill, whose maiden name is Michaelson, suffers from a rare disorder called 'Michaelson's Syndrome,' which affects all members of her family. This syndrome causes the brain to turn very slowly into something resembling pureed spinach. By the time she is thirty she will remember nothing of these unhappy events, for she will have devolved to a rather primitive, excrement-throwing stage. Whatever should they do?"

All that was required of Mrs. Ann was the rallying cry: a country house! Many hours were spent trying to find new awful tidings for Jill and Bill, and as those familiar with the effects of marijuana know, even the punctual are carried away on a stream of warped time perceptions. One rock-and-roll song takes about an hour to play, whereas a movement of a symphony is over in fifteen seconds. I felt that time had a form—the form of a chiffon scarf floating aimlessly down a large water slide; or that it was oblong but slippery, like an oiled football. I got home late, having forgotten to do the shopping. Since I had freely opted to be Thorne's housewife, he was perfectly justified in getting angry with me. My problem was, he thought I was having an affair.

It is one thing to tell your husband that you are sleeping with another man, and it is quite another to tell him that from the very instant of your meeting you have been under the influence of a mind-altering substance, no matter how mild. An astonishing confession next to which the admission of an afternoon or two in the arms of another man is nothing. Nothing!

What was I to do? My only real talent in life appeared to be getting high, and I was wonderful at it. Ostensibly I was supposed to be nurturing a talent for drawing—everyone had a skill, it was assumed. Every day I went upstairs to our attic room, lit a joint, and drew tiny, incoherent, and highly detailed black and white pictures. This was not my idea of an occupation. It was hardly my idea of a hobby. Of course it is a well-known fact that drawing while high is always fun which only made it more clear to me that my true vocation lay in getting stoned.

And so when dinner was late, when I was late, when I had forgotten to do something I had said I would do, Thorne liked to get into a snit, but he was terrified of getting furious with me. After all, my role was to look sort of dangerous. In some ways, Thorne treated me with the respectful and careful handling you might give to something you suspect is a pipe bomb: he didn't want to tempt fate because the poor thing was in some ways enraptured with me and he was afraid that if he got mad enough, I might disappear. That was the way the scales of our marriage were balanced. When he looked as if he were about to shout, I would either get a very dangerous look in my eyes, or I would make him laugh, which was one of my prime functions in his life. The other was to behave in public.

Since I was stoned all the time, I tried in all ways to behave like Queen Victoria. Thus I probably appeared to be a little cracked. At public functions I smiled and was mute—no one knew that at home I was quite a little chatterbox. The main form of socializing on campus was the dinner party. I found these pretty funny—of course I was high and didn't know the difference. Thorne found them pretty dull, so I tried to liven them up for him. If we were seated together at dinner, I would smile at the person opposite and then do something to Thorne under the table. I tended, at these parties, to smile a great deal. This unnerved Thorne. He wore, under his party expression, a grimace that might have been caused by constant prayer, the prayer that I would not say something I had said at home. That I would not talk about how a black transvestite hooker should be sent as a present to the president of the college for his birthday. He prayed that I would not say about this gift: "With my little inheritance and Thorne's salary I think we could certainly afford it." Or I would not discuss the ways in which I felt the chairman of the history department looked like an anteater, or, on the subject of ants, how I felt his wife would react to being rolled in honey and set upon by South American fire ants. I did think that Professor X stole women's clothing out of the townie laundromat and went through the streets late at night in a flowered housecoat. I knew why Professor Y should not be left alone with his own infant son, and so on. But I behaved like a perfect angel and from time to time sent Thorne a look that made him shake, just to keep him on his toes.

I actually spoke once. This was at a formal dinner at the chairman of the department's house. This dinner party was so unusually dull that even through a glaze of marijuana I was bored. Thorne looked as if he were drowning. I myself began to itch. When I could stand it no longer I excused myself and went to the bathroom where I lit the monster joint I carried in my evening bag and took a few hits. This was Lionel's super-fine Colombian loco-weed and extremely effective. When I came downstairs I felt all silvery. The chairman of the department's wife was talking about her niece, Allison, who was an accomplished young equestrienne. At the mention of horses, I spoke up. I remembered something about horses I had figured out high. Lionel Browning called these insights "marijuana moments"—things you like to remember when you are not stoned. Since no one had ever heard me say very much, everyone stopped to listen.

"Man's spatial relationship to the horse is one of the most confusing and deceptive in the world," I heard myself say. "You are either sitting on top of one, or standing underneath one, and therefore it is impossible to gauge in any meaningful way exactly how big a horse is in relationship to you. This is not," I added with fierce emphasis, "like a man inside a cathedral."

I then shut up. There was a long silence. I meditated on what I had said which was certainly the most interesting thing anyone had said. Thorne's eyes seemed about to pop. There was not a sound. People had stopped eating. I looked around the table, gave a beautiful, unfocused smile, and went back to my dinner.

Finally, the chairman of the department's wife said: "That's very interesting, Ann." And the conversation closed above my head, leaving me happy to rattle around in my own altered state.

Later, at home, Thorne said: "Whatever made you say what you said at dinner tonight?"

I said, in a grave voice: "It is something I have always believed."

The nice thing about being high all the time is that life suspends itself in front of you endlessly, like telephone poles on a highway. Without plans you have the feeling that things either will never change, or will arrange themselves somehow someday.

A look around the campus did not fill the heart of this tender bride with visions of a rosy adult future. It was clear who was having all the fun and it was not the grown-ups. Thorne and I were the youngest faculty couple, and this gave us—I mean me—a good vantage point. A little older than us were couples with worn-out cars, sick children, and debts. If they were not saddled with these things, they had independent incomes and were saddled with attitudes. Then they got older and were seen kissing the spouses of others at parties, or were found, a pair of unassorted spouses, under a pile of coats on a bed at New Year's Eve parties. Then they got even older, and the strife of their marriages gave them the stony affection battle comrades have for one another.

There were marriages that seemed propped up with tooth-picks, and ones in which the wife was present but function-less, like a vestigial organ. Then the husband, under the strain of being both father and more to little Emily, Matthew, and Tabitha plus teaching a full course load, was forced to have an affair with a graduate student in Boston whom he could see only every other weekend.

The thought of Thorne and my becoming any of these peo-ple was so frightful that I had no choice but to get immediately high. Something would either occur to me, or nothing would happen. Meanwhile, time drifted by in the company of Lionel Browning—a fine fellow and a truly great pothead for whom I had not one particle of sexual feeling. He was my perfect pal. Was this cheating? I asked myself. Well, I had to admit, it sort of was. Thorne did not know how much time I spent with him, but then Linnie was soon to graduate, so I had to get him while I could, so to speak.

In the spring, Thorne went off to a convention of the Historical Society and I went on a dope run to Boston with Linnie. I looked forward to this adventure. It did not seem likely that life would bring me many more offers of this sort. The purity of my friendship with Linnie was never tainted by the well-known number of motels that littered the road from school to Boston. Sex was never our mission.

We paid a visit to a dealer named Marv (he called himself Uncle Marv) Fenrich, who was somewhat of a legend. The legend had it that he had once been very brilliant, but that speed—his drug of choice—had turned his brain into shaving cream and now he was fit only to deal grass to college boys. He also dealt speed to more sinister campus types, and he had tried to con Linnie into this lucrative sideline. But Linnie wanted only quality marijuana and Uncle Marv respected him, although it irked him that Linnie was not interested. He sold what he called "The Uncle Marv Exam Special— Tailored to the Needs of the College Person." This was a box containing two 5 milligram Dexamyls, a Dexamyl Spansule (15 mgs), two Benzedrines (5 mg), and something he called an "amphetamine football"—a large, olive-green pill which he claimed was pure speed coated with Vitamin B_{12}. On the shelves of his linen closet were jar upon hospital-size jar of pills. But his heart, if not the rest of his metabolism, was in grass, and he never shut up.

"Man," he said, "now this particular reefer is very sublime, really very sublime. It is the country club of grass, mellow and

rich. A very handsome high can be gotten off this stuff. Now
my own personal favorite cocktail is to take two or three nice
dexies, wash them down with some fine whiskey or it could be
Sterno or your mother's French perfume, it makes no difference whatsoever, and then light up a huge monster reefer of
the very best quality and fall on the floor thanking God in
many languages. This is my own recipe for a very good time. I
like to share these warm happy times with others. Often Uncle
Marv suggests you do a popper or two if you feel unmotivated
by any of the above. Or snap one under the nose of a loved
friend. Believe me, the drugstore has a lot to offer these days.
Now a hundred or so of those little Romilar pills make you
writhe and think insects are crawling all over your body—
some people like this sort of thing very deeply. I myself find it
a cheap thrill. Say, Linnie, have you authentic college kids
gotten into mescaline yet? Very attractive stuff. Yes, you may
say that it is for people with no imagination, but think of it
this way: if you have no imagination, a Swiss pharmaceutical
company will supply one for you. Isn't that wonderful what
modern science does? Let me tell you, this stuff is going to be
very big. Uncle Marv is going to make many sublime shekels
off this stuff as soon as he can set it up right. You just wait
and see. Uncle Marv says: the streets of Boston and Cambridge are going to be stacked with little college boys and girls
hyperventilating and having visions. Now this lysergic acid is
also going to be very big, very big. God bless the Swiss! Now,
Linnie," he began rooting in various desk drawers. "Now,
Linnie, how about some reds for all those wired-up college
boys and girls to calm down after exams? I personally feel
that reds go very well after a little speed abuse and I should
know. Calm you down, take the reptile right out of you.
Uncle Marv is so fond of these sublime red tens." He paused.
"Seconal," he said rather coldly to me, since it was clear even
to a person who was out of his mind that I did not know what

he was talking about. "I like to see a person taking reds. This is a human person, a person unafraid to admit that he or she is *very nervous*. You don't want any? Well, all right. But you and this authentic college girl have not come to pass the evening in idle drug chatter. This is business. Reefer for Linnie, many shekels for Uncle Marv. Now, Linnie, this reefer in particular I want you to taste is very sublime. You and this authentic college girl must try some this very instant. Now this is Colombian loco-weed of the highest order. Of Colombian distinction and extremely handsome. I also have some horse tranquilizers, by the way. Interested? Extremely sublime. They make you lie down on the floor and whimper for help and companionship. Uncle Marv is very fond of these interesting new pills."

He cleared a space on his messy kitchen table and proceeded to roll several absolutely perfect joints. It was extremely sublime grass, and Linnie bought a kilo of it.

"Linnie, it will not fail you," Uncle Marv said. "Only the best, from me to you." Linnie paid up, and Uncle Marv gave us each a bennie for a present, which we were very glad to have on the long ride home.

When Thorne came back from his conference, the axe, which had been poised so delicately over the back of my neck, fell. This marked the end of my old life, and the beginning of the new. Thorne had called me from Chicago—he had called all night—and I had not been home.

"You are sleeping with Lionel Browning," he said.

"I never laid a hand on him," I said.

"That's an interesting locution, Ann," said Thorne. "Do you just lie there and let him run his grubby undergraduate hands all over you?"

This was of course my cue. "Yes," I said. "I often lie there and let almost any undergraduate run his hands all over me. Often faculty is invited, like your colleague Jack Saks. Often the chairman of the department's wife pops over and she runs her hands all over me too."

The effects of the beautiful joint I had smoked only an hour and a half ago were beginning to wane. I was getting a headache. I thought about the sweet little stash I kept in my lingerie drawer—all the grass I smoked at home tasted vaguely of sachet. I was longing to go upstairs where, underneath my socks, I had a little lump of African hash. I saw my future before me—a very depressing vision. I was fifty. Grown children. Going to the hairdresser to have my hair frosted. Doing some genteel work or other—I couldn't think what. Wearing a knit dress—the sort worn by the wife of the president of the college. Calling grimy boys from pay phones: "Hello, hello? Kenny? Steve? This is Mrs. Speizer calling. Do you have anything for me?"

There I would be in my proper hairdo. Facing change of life and still a total pothead. Locking the bathroom door behind me to toke up. By then Thorne would be the chairman of his department somewhere.

"That wife of mine," he would say—of course he only spoke this way in my fantasies—"does say the oddest things. Can't keep track of where that mind of hers is meandering to. Goes out at odd hours and what funny boys she gets to do the lawn work. I can't imagine where she gets them from."

In fact, this was the most depressing thought I had ever had. If you stay high enough you never wonder what will become of you. A large joint was waiting in my jacket pocket. How I longed to smoke it. Somewhere near me was adult life: I knew it. I could feel it breathing down my neck. Professor's

wife smokes dope constantly must see shrink. Must grow up.
Must find out why she cannot be straight. Why she refuses to
enter the adult world. And so on. And Thorne—much sym-
pathy for Thorne—for example, the chairman of the department's wife: "Dear Thorne, you poor thing! All alone in that
house with a drug addict! When Ann has been sedated why
don't you come over and have dinner with us and our lovely
niece Allison and after Ann has been committed to a mental
institution, you and Allison can establish a meaningful and
truly adult relationship."

The thing that divides the children from the adults is
that children know it's us against them—how right they
are—and adults are children who grew up and are comfortable being *them*. Two terrible images flashed before me.
One was that life was like an unruly horse that rears up
and kicks you in the head. And the other was that my life was
like a pane of glass being carried around by a nervous and
incompetent person who was bound to let it slip and shatter into zillions of pieces on the pavement. My futureless
life, besides being shattered and rearing up, unwound endlessly before me. What was around for me to be? There
did not seem to be very much of anything. Suddenly I felt
a rush of jaunty courage, the kind you feel when everything has bottomed out and just about every old thing
is lost.

"Thorne," I said. "I smoke marijuana unceasingly and always have. What do you think of that?"

"Incessantly," said Thorne.

"Thorne," I said. "I have been stoned from the first minute
you laid eyes on me and I am stoned now."

He regarded me for a moment. "You mean, you came to
my class high?" Thorne said. "And you're high now?"

"Yes," I said. "I was stoned in your class and I am stoned

right now but not as stoned as I want to be. So I am going to take this great big gigantic reefer out of my pocket and light it up and I am going to share it with you."

He looked shocked.

"You can get in jail for smoking that stuff, Ann," he said in an awed voice.

"An interesting locution, Thorne," I said. He stopped looking awed and began to look rather keen and hungry. I realized with a sudden jolt of happiness that I could very well change my husband's life in one easy step.

"Take this thing and inhale it," I said.

"How can I when I don't smoke?" Thorne said.

"Make an effort. Try hard and be careful," I said. "Go slow and don't exhale for a long time."

"How long?" Thorne asked.

"Oh, a half an hour or so." He inhaled successfully several times. In a little while he was high as a kite.

"My," he said, "this certainly is an interesting substance. I feel I've been standing here for a few centuries. My hands are cold and my mouth is dry. Are these symptoms?"

For an hour Thorne went from room to room having impressions. He was having a wonderful time. Finally, he sat down.

"Were you stoned on our wedding day?" he asked.

"I'm afraid so," I said.

"On our honeymoon?"

"I'm afraid so."

"I see," said Thorne. "In other words, you're like this all the time."

I said more or less, mostly more.

"In other words," said Thorne, "since you are like this all the time, you have no idea what it's like to be with me when you're not like this."

That seemed logical to me.

"In other words," Thorne said, "you have no idea what it's like to be with me when you aren't like this."

I said that sounded very like his previous other words, and that such a thought had never occurred to me.

"This is terrible, Ann," said Thorne. "It isn't normal. Of course, this stuff is pretty interesting and all, but you can't be stoned all the time."

"I can," I said.

"Yes, but it must be wrong. There must be something terribly wrong, don't you think?"

"Actually, no," I said.

"But, Ann, in other words, this is not normal reality. You have not been perceiving normal reality. How long has it been, Ann, since you actually perceived normal reality?"

"This is normal reality, silly," I said.

"Yes, well, but I mean I'm sure there is some reason why it's not right to be this way all the time."

"There may be, but I can't think of it. Besides," I added, "you seem to be having a swell old time."

"That cannot be gainsaid," said Thorne.

"Or cannot not be gainsaid."

"What does that mean, anyway?" said Thorne. "But never mind. The fact is that if you've been high all this time, we don't know each other at all, really."

"What," I said, thinking with sudden longing of the hashish upstairs, "is knowable?"

"An interesting point," said Thorne. "Maybe in the open knowableness of things their sheer knowableness is obscured. In other words, light darkening light, if you see what I mean."

I did see. I looked at my husband with great affection, realizing that he had possibilities I had not counted on.

"What about your affair with Lionel Browning?" Thorne said. "Is that knowable?"

"Yes," I said. "Lionel Browning is responsible only for the very substance that has put you in this state of mind, see?"

"I do see," Thorne said. "I see. In other words, you sit around and get high together."

"Often we stand up and get high together."

"And I as a professor can never join you since that would be undignified, right?"

"Right."

"Well, then, in honor of Lionel and in the interests of further study, let's have a little more of this stuff, okay?"

"A very good idea," I said.

"Yes," said Thorne, stretching out on the couch. "Let's carry this one step further."

"An interesting locution," I said. "I wonder how it works. In what way can a step be carried?"

Thorne sat up. He looked puzzled. "It must go like this: the step is the province of the foot, without which there can be no step. The foot is carried by the body, but the action of the step is carried by foot. Therefore the step is to the foot as a baby is to its mother. And so it can be said that the foot is the mother of the step, or rather, the step is the potential baby of the foot."

I thought about that for a very long time.

"Say, Ann," Thorne said. "Where's the more we're supposed to have?"

"It's illegal, Thorne," I said. "We could get in jail for simply being in the same room with it."

"Get it if you have it," Thorne said.

I brought down a bag of Linnie's top quality and my lump of hash. This I scraped with our sharpest kitchen knife and sprinkled deftly on the unrolled reefer. I rolled wonderfully.

Thorne was impressed, and he was intrigued by watching me do something I had obviously done millions of times but not in front of him.

"You're awfully good at that," he said.

"Years of practice," I said. "Now, Thorne, why have you never told me how much Lionel Browning looks like me?"

"Because he does *not* look like you," said Thorne. "You have the same loafers, that's all."

"We are virtually identical," I said.

"Ann, this mind-impairing substance has impaired your mind. Lionel Browning and you look nothing alike. Now are you going to roll those things all night or are you going to smoke them?"

The thing about history is, most people just live through it. You never know what moment may turn out to be of profound historical significance. When you are meandering near the stream of current events, you do not know when you have dipped your toe into the waters of significance. I like to think that as I passed that joint to my husband, a new era opened. The decade was fairly new, and just about everything was about to happen. In what other era could a nice young thing pass a marijuana cigarette to her straight-laced husband?

In those days potheads liked to try to track down their fellow heads. Everyone had a list of suspects. William Blake was on everyone's list. On Linnie's list was Gerard Manley Hopkins. It amused him inexhaustibly to imagine the Jesuit father smoking dope and writing in sprung rhythm. I myself could not imagine any straight person writing those poems and as I watched a happy, glazed expression take possession of my husband's features, I had cause to think of my favorite Hopkins poem—"The Windhover"—which contains the line, "my heart in hiding/Stirred for a bird,—the achieve of, the mastery of the thing!"

I felt full of achievement and mastery—Thorne being the victim and beneficiary of both. Getting him stoned was a definite achievement of some sort or other.

I said to Thorne: "What do you think of it?"

"It produces a strange and extremely endearing form of cerebral energy," he said.

"Yes," I sighed in agreement. "Wonderful, isn't it?"

"It produces unhealthy mental excitement," Thorne said. Suddenly I was full of optimism and hope for the future.

"Oh, Thorne," I said in a happy voice. "Isn't this fun?"

And as Thorne has frequently pointed out, that very well could have been the slogan for the years to come.

Family Happiness

Everyone in Polly's family was odd in some way or other. Her mother, Wendy, got everybody's name wrong, and once she got it wrong, she stood by it. For example she called Douglas Stern "Derwood" and had for fifteen years. She could never remember the names of Polly's school friends (unless they were the children of her friends) and referred to them as "the little Underwood girl," "the little Rice girl," and "the Harbison girl"—Wendy had not liked the Harbison girl at all, and so she did not put "little" in front of her name. Wendy also got the names of famous people wrong. She did not call Pablo Picasso "Carlos" as her family joked she did, but she might as well have. Her real name was Hortensia, and her sisters—they had been the Mendoza sisters—were Carmelita, called Lila; Hildegarde, called Hattie; and Graciela, who was not, as one might have expected, called Grace but Nancy. This explained, it was felt, Wendy's problem getting names straight.

Polly was flanked by two difficult brothers. The younger, Henry, Jr., had one passion in life and that was aerodynamics. As a child he had stayed in his room streamlining kites and making model airplanes. He had been allergic as a child to a great many ubiquitous substances such as cow's milk, dust, and feathers. He had shocked the family by going to engineering school—the Solo-Millers did not know any engineers and did not know what sort of people they were. At engineering school he had met a Czech girl named Andreya, and they had gotten married. Andreya's English was either scanty or she was shy. She rarely spoke. Polly said that Henry and Andreya communicated algebraically and did not need normal speech. Andreya, who was also an engineer, was a vegetarian, a fact neither she nor Henry had bothered to tell anyone. For several years as they watched her pass up the roast beef and the spring lamb, the family felt she was trying to starve herself, although she was always as healthy as a horse. A lovely plate of vegetables could easily have been provided her, if anyone had known.

Polly's older brother was Paul, also known to his mother as Polly. And since Polly's father was Henry, Sr., this gave Wendy only two names to get straight. Paul had always been solitary and cranky. He was said to be very brilliant, but since he was so silent no one had ever heard him say a brilliant thing. Like his father he was a lawyer so it was felt that his partners got the benefit of the brilliance he possessed. As for Henry, Jr., who was also said to be very brilliant, no one except Andreya understood his field. Paul should have been married but was not. He did not show any signs of being homosexual—in the Solo-Miller family that meant taking more of an interest in the theatre or opera than was socially required. In fact he had a consort—a woman slightly older than himself who owned a fashionable antique store and had

twin teenage daughters. He had not brought this woman—
Wendy referred to her as such—to the family, but they were
often seen at the symphony, which was Paul's passion, sharing
an opened score.

Polly's father was rather mad. He believed all food should
be washed before being cooked, even eggs in the shell. No one
paid much attention to this except for Polly, who as a teenager had once put a chicken into the washing machine. The
food at the Solo-Millers was generally wonderful. Thus
Henry, Sr., was constantly lied to. He was told that things
which had not been washed had. He had many crotchets
about nutrition and was always told that the butter on his
plate was margarine and that every vegetable was verifiably
organic.

As for Polly, Polly was marvelous. The family doted on
her, but no one paid much attention to her. She was the solid,
normal one—friendly, cheerful, good-tempered. She had no
oddities at all and reminded her family what they would have
been like if they hadn't been so unusual—a word Polly felt
had only a pejorative connotation. She was good-looking—all
the Solo-Millers were—a good cook, good at games, could
write nonsense verse, remembered everyone's name, got the
shy to speak and the timid to come forward. Polly was married to a man named Henry Demarest who was also a lawyer
and they had two children. The joke was that Polly had married a lawyer named Henry so as not to confuse poor Wendy
who got everything so screwed up.

This was the family that people without family, or with a
family in trouble, or a family that no longer worked, looked
to. And looking to the Solo-Millers made people feel how
unfair life is. They had money, good looks, and a sense of
cohesion. They behaved like an exclusive tribe, and it was felt
that the Solo-Millers preferred the company of their fellow

Solo-Millers to that of anyone else. Wendy's sisters were all considered part of this tribe. The Solo-Millers drew people into their circle, but the family, of course, came first.

Everything about them looked attractive, including their oddities. And so even though Paul was abnormally silent and would not reveal his lady friend, and Henry, Jr.'s wife would not speak English, and Wendy got everything wrong and Henry, Sr., had an opinion on every subject, the family was together rather a lot.

They gathered for Sunday brunch, for birthdays and anniversaries, on New Year's Day, on Christmas Eve as well as Easter Sunday. They were an old, old Jewish family of the sort that is more identifiably old American than Jewish. They gathered at Passover but not at Chanukah, and they went to synagogue twice a year on the two High Holy days. On Yom Kippur they did not fast but had family lunch in the afternoon.

They had their Thanksgiving turkey, Easter ham, Christmas goose, and Passover capon off English Victorian plates. Their silver was old Danish. They liked great big cut crystal glasses and cut crystal wine glasses. Proper wine glasses seemed precious and rather arriviste to them.

On an early spring day, Polly sat in a big leather chair in her father's study. The Solo-Millers had a duplex apartment the study of which was on the second floor. Polly could faintly hear the sound of her children, Pete, six, and Dee-Dee, four, downstairs annoying their father and grandfather. The Sunday paper was on Polly's lap. She had skimmed its contents and was now staring out the window, past the big china bowl of lilies of the valley that Wendy had set on a table in the corner. She was finishing her coffee and waiting until it was the right time to call her best beloved. Polly was having an affair with a man her own age, a painter by the name of Lincoln Bennett. She dialed his number, let it ring once, hung up, and dialed again. It was her signal. He picked up instantly.

"Yellow dog," he said.

"Hello, Linky," Polly said. "It's only me."

"Only you, huh?" Lincoln said. "I keep getting telephone calls all day long none of which are only you, if only they were. I assume you're in the study, right?"

"Yes."

"And the lawyer and the little grubs are downstairs."

"Yes," said Polly.

"Then, what, beautiful darling, is our schedule?"

"Well, I've come up with another seminar downtown."

"Hmm," said Lincoln. "The fictitious seminar ploy. It's a good thing none of them understand what your job is. Can you get down here by three?"

"In the neighborhood of."

"All right, swell Yellow. Bring me some leftover salmon, will you?"

Lincoln was the only person Polly knew who called her by her given name, which was Dora. He called her any number of things as well—he made them up as he went along. He called her Doe, Dot, Dottie, Dorrit, Doreen, and Dor, which had been corrupted into Dog and then turned to Yellow Dog and Yellow. Lincoln had known Henry, Jr., since grammar school, and the basis of their friendship was kite flying. Many attempts had been made to draw Lincoln into the Solo-Miller orbit. His grandmother, in fact, and Polly's grandmother had been friends. But Lincoln was not much of a fan of the idea of families, and he found the Solo-Millers, as an artifact, rather antipathetic. They were smug, he felt. If you found them enchanting you said they were eccentric. If you did not, they were annoying. The Solo-Millers did not properly appreciate their beautiful and remarkable Polly, Lincoln felt. Polly was different: privilege had not made her Olympian and snooty like her brother Paul, or arrogant and sulky like Henry, Jr. Catering to those temperaments had made her kind, tender-hearted, and innocent in her feelings. As to the Solo-Millers, they would have liked to collect him. Wendy, of whom he was not fond, had always liked him. "That nice Leonard Bender," she always said. "So attractive and so well behaved, for a painter."

Polly had remet him at one of his openings. She and her husband Henry and her brother Henry had gone to Lincoln's fancy gallery and sipped white wine while admiring his paint-ings. He was, in fact, very talented. Furthermore, he was very attractive: tall, lanky, boyish, with an unsmiling face, plain glasses, and a thick shock of straight hair that hung over his forehead. He had a big, almost pouty mouth and, when he smiled, an extremely silly grin. He was wearing the sort of clothes a young fisherman might wear, or they might have been painter's clothes: a turtleneck sweater, heavy tweed trousers, and heavy shoes that seemed to be oiled and which laced. Polly could tell at once that he was rather loony. And, she was not surprised when, upon introduction, he kissed her on the mouth.

"Oh, I'm sorry," he said. "I thought you were someone else." He smiled a rattled smile.

Polly had been married to Henry Demarest for eight years. He was big and handsome. His short hair waved no matter how it was cut, and he was traditional in his clothing on which he liked to spend a lot of money His underwear was made for him of pima cotton. He was a perfect husband—so like the rest of Polly's family that she had little to get used to. Her

present home was a slightly less grand edition of her childhood dwelling. Her children's childhood was a replica of her
own. Henry's sense of what life was like was very Solo-Miller-
like. She had moved from one family to another and often
hardly noticed the difference. Lincoln's kiss had rather a dramatic effect. She felt it all the way to the bottoms of her
feet.

Before she left she went right up to him.

"I want to buy one of those oil on paper pictures," she
said.

"I'm afraid you'll have to come to my studio," Lincoln
said. "Would you like to come this minute, or you could come
tomorrow."

"Tomorrow," Polly said. "What time?"

"As soon as possible," he said. "I'm always there. Here's
my card. The address is on it."

The next day she appeared at his studio at noon. It was the
only time she had, but it troubled her to appear at lunchtime.
When he opened the door, Polly suddenly kissed him on the
mouth.

"Oh, I'm sorry," she said. "I thought you were somone
else." Her heart was pounding. She could not imagine what
had taken possession of her.

"I knew you'd be here for lunch," Lincoln said. In the back
of his big, neat studio were his living quarters: a bed, a
wooden table, six chairs, a desk, and an armchair. The table
had been set for lunch, which melted Polly's heart. Lunch
consisted of bread, cheese, a bottle of wine, a bunch of
grapes, and a plate of cookies. After lunch they went directly
to bed as if everything had been arranged beforehand.

They spent the afternoon in bed. Polly called her office and invented an excuse. It amazed her with what perfect ease she lied. She called her housekeeper and invented another excuse. By the end of the afternoon, they were both in love. They giggled and laughed and played like children, and when it was time for Polly to go home, they immediately set up a schedule. Both of them were orderly. Polly would call Lincoln at a certain time on the three days a week she went to her office. On her home days she would call him a little earlier, after Henry and the children had gone off to work and school. They would meet as often as possible and, if they were ever seen, Polly would say that Lincoln was painting her portrait as a present to either Henry or her parents and, if it was ever necessary to produce such a work, Lincoln would dash one off.

Polly was, in fact, a demon organizer. How else could she have tended two children, run her household, organized her housekeeper, run a social life, pleased a husband who required some attention, participated in her family life, and had a lover, too?

As to Polly's job, her mother could never keep straight what it was. She could understand "lawyer" and "professor" and "designer" or even Henry's and Andreya's jobs, which were "aeronautical engineers." But "Assistant Co-Ordinator for the Evaluation of Pilot Reading Methods" stumped her. What Polly did was to survey and evaluate every new reading project available to schools and assess them. She worked for an educational corporation that produced information for the Board of Education. Wendy thought this was a very strange job, but then she did not understand jobs that were neither glamorous nor power producing, or, at the very least, interesting to describe. Furthermore, Wendy was old school, and in her unexamined heart she did not believe women should work —unless they were, say, the head of a large cosmetics company. Nice women *volunteered*. When she thought of women who actually worked for a living, Wendy thought of librarians, or the lingerie fitters at Saks Fifth Avenue, or of Madame Rubenstein. That Polly had gotten herself what sounded like a boring, bureaucratic job puzzled her, but then Polly had always been the stolid member of the family.

This job gave her considerable leeway. It produced a number of fictitious seminars in Lincoln's neighborhood and once produced an actual business trip—three days away with Lincoln in Vermont. Her colleagues were not the sort of people Henry Demarest would ever have socialized with, so he would never discover that she had not been on a business trip.

After her call to Lincoln, Polly sat down to her parents' table with a light heart. The fact that she loved Lincoln and Lincoln loved her had the same effect a secret and longed-for toy has on a child: she could not get over that it was now hers.

Nothing had deviated on the table for as long as Polly could remember. At each person's place was a small glass of fresh orange juice. There were breakfast plates decorated with cornflowers, pheasants, and vines. There were heavy white plates of smoked salmon, sliced tomatoes, onion, and lemon wedges. There was a plate of cream cheese that had been molded in an ornamental pudding mold; and silver baskets of toast points; and cobalt blue glass dishes of capers. At Wendy's end was the big silver coffee pot, the silver pot of hot milk, and the big silver sugar dish filled with lump sugar that was served with silver tongs. The cups they drank from on Sunday mornings were eggshell porcelain decorated with birds. These cups annoyed Polly and always had. She liked a great big cup of coffee, a like that was not shared by any member of her family except Lincoln whom she included, because she loved him so, in her family feelings. Those fragile cups kept the coffee too hot to drink at once, but if you dawdled at all, the coffee became instantly stone cold.

Around the table were Wendy, Henry, Sr., Pete, Dee-Dee, Henry Demarest, and three blank places for Paul, Henry, Jr., and Andreya. Then there was Polly.

As he did every Sunday, Henry, Sr., began by disapproving of the smoked salmon.

"The exact equivalent of smoking cigarettes," he said. "Polly, I really can't imagine how you can feed that stuff to Pete and Dee-Dee."

"Daddy, this salmon is very lightly smoked. Mother and I have been all over New York comparing, and this salmon is the most lightly cured and the most lightly smoked. It's barely smoked at all."

"That's worse," said Henry, Sr. "Fish flesh is the ideal breeding ground for parasites. At least smoking kills them."

"Yes, Daddy. But this is adequately smoked, although not smoked enough to be harmful." She passed the silver basket to her children. "Don't grab, darling," she said to Pete. "When something is passed to you, you take it gently."

"I am a woolly beast," said Pete. "Woolly, woolly, woolly."

"Even a woolly beast can take a piece of toast without grabbing," said Polly.

"No, they can't," said Pete. "They have great big woolly paws and they have to grab. Woolly, woolly, woolly."

"Stop that at once," said Polly, but sweetly. She could not help it but she loved when her children got out of hand. In her secret heart, she was on their side and she longed for Henry Demarest's business trips so that she and the children could eat nursery food around the wooden kitchen table. Polly liked to make shepherd's pie, lamb stew, mashed potatoes, junket, stewed figs with cream, hush puppies, hermits, and rice pudding. For Henry she served a more elaborate cuisine. He liked complicated food: stuffed breast of veal, carpetbagger steak, fresh ham with pistachio, all of which Polly was happy to provide, but her favorite time of the year was late February, with lots of sleety, messy weather, Henry in Boston or Dallas or San Francisco, and she and the children being silly and having dinner. Her children knew instinctively that their mother was almost helpless to stop them, so when they misbehaved, they did so delicately.

"Woolly, woolly, woolly," whispered Dee-Dee, whose real name was Claire.

"That's quite enough, you two," said Henry Demarest. He loved his children dearly, but he found them trying at meals. On the weeknights Polly sat with Pete and Dee-Dee while they had their supper and then had dinner with Henry. Henry liked to apportion time: an hour after he came home—if he was not working late—to have his drink and let his children crawl all over him. Then he liked to put them to bed, kiss them goodnight, and sit down to a good meal in the dining room with Polly.

Pete and Dee-Dee always obeyed their father, but whenever Polly looked at them, she saw that they were mouthing the word "woolly" over and over again, and dissolving into soundless giggles.

At these brunches the family was encouraged to speak of family matters, current events, and to share moments of their professional lives. As children, Paul, Polly, and Henry, Jr., had been taught the art of dinner table conversation, but it was practiced only by the senior Solo-Millers, Polly, and Henry Demarest, who was a master at it.

Before the conversation got underway, the front hall door was heard to open, and Paul, Henry, Jr., and Andreya appeared with Henry and Andreya's dog. They were all red-cheeked from the cold. A great deal of kissing and handshaking took place and then all got down to eating and talking.

As always happened, the table divided into the silent half and the legal half, with Polly in the middle. Henry Demarest and Henry, Sr., discussed a point of law, referring to Paul from time to time. Paul nodded, said yes, or no, or quite—a term he and his father employed for noncommittal response —and buttered his toast.

Henry and Andreya's dog was a Bluetick Hound which Wendy had thought for several years was called a fleahound. Then she had thought that the dog had ticks and had banned it from the house. When it was explained to her that this was a breed and not a condition, she relented, but she did not like dogs except in the country when they belonged to other people. Both she and Henry, Sr., felt that they brought awful things into the house from the street on their paws. This dog was called Kirby. Wendy, of course, called it Kelly.

That Henry, Jr., fed this animal bits of smoked salmon under the table made Wendy want to scream, and when Andreya did it, it made her want to jump up and down, but she was silent. Andreya could be spoken sharply about, but not sharply spoken to. Both Henry and Andreya knew this, and so Andreya mostly did the under the table feeding. Henry was too intent on eating to notice his mother trying to get his eye. He was doing something else she found objectionable. He and Polly called it "building a sandwich." They liked to put layer upon layer upon layer of things on a piece of toast and then eat it in two bites. Wendy, Henry, Sr., and Paul found this disgusting. Polly adored it. When she was alone she did the same thing, but never in front of her children who might easily pick it up, as dogs pick things up on their paws, and bring it to disturb their grandmother's house.

Soon the legal half of the table extended to the table at large. Henry, Jr., spoke at length about a glider he and Andreya were going to build. A good part of this recitation was numerical. Andreya nodded energetically, her eyes bright with the effort to understand. Paul asked two direct questions about the economics of the aerospace industry and Henry Demarest told a complicated anecdote about one of his firm's aerospace industry clients. Wendy misreported something she had read in the paper about what she called "the jet promotion engine" and then Pete and Dee-Dee who had been giggling silently all through lunch became crazed with boredom and were excused from the table. They were sent, as they were sent every Sunday, into the library where they could read picture books or take all the cushions off the chairs and sofas and build fortresses. On Sunday mornings Wendy took everything breakable out of the library so that the children could play to their hearts' content.

To open up the conversation, Wendy asked Henry, Jr., about someone she had met roughly six dozen times.

"And how is that nice friend of yours, Bill Friedrich?" she said.

"Tom Friedrich," said Henry, Jr.

"I said Tom, didn't I?" Wendy said.

"You said Bill."

"Well, I think of him as Bill, but I always try to say Tom," Wendy said. "Are you feeding Kelly under the table?"

She knew that Andreya was in fact feeding Kirby under the table and every Sunday she used this method to get her to stop. It never worked.

"Kirby," said Henry, Jr. "And I'm not feeding him. Poll, pass the toast. And pass the cream cheese. No, wait a second. It's all on your side of the table. Build me a sandwich, will you?"

As Polly layered Henry's sandwich, the conversation came her way: equal attention was a firm Solo-Miller rule. Pete and Dee-Dee figured as her part of the conversation. Polly had used to wonder if no one ever asked her anything about herself because she was just a girl, and the answer was no. No one ever asked her anything because she was so normal. She had graduated near the top of her class at a good school, had worked for a year as a reading teacher, gotten engaged and married to Henry Demarest, taken a honeymoon trip to France, set up house seventeen blocks from her parents, gotten a master's degree, and eventually produced Pete and Dee-Dee. She had not stayed unmarried nor had she married someone who would not speak English. She had not gotten divorced, or disagreed violently with anyone, or entertained an odd idea or notion. She had never given anyone the slightest pause.

When her part in the conversation had been satisfied, Polly stood up. "Well, you all," she said. "I've got another of those interminable seminars and I must dash. Henry, don't let the children eat another thing until I get home except for a glass of milk and a cookie at four. Goodbye, everyone."

When she went to kiss her children, she found that they had taken off all the couch pillows and had themselves fallen into a heap. They were such darling children, so adorable, so kind to one another. They had fallen to sleep like kittens. In the elevator she was careful not to reveal to the elevator man, who had known her since she was a teenager, her immense relief.

Lincoln's studio was on a side street in a row of studios built for artists in the twenties. It was a narrow, cobbled street with warehouses on the other side. It was impossible to walk down this street without coming upon a stray cat. Some were feral and raced away, and some were lonely and followed you, crying mournfully. These lonely cats brought Polly almost to tears. She was tender on the subject of animals, but the cats reminded her of herself: so willing, so hungry for love.

Polly was used to understanding but not to being understood. In her family it had been her lot to sympathize with Henry if Paul was cruel to him, or with Paul if Henry hit him. She brought breakfast trays to her mother on those days when Wendy stayed in bed, and she had a drink waiting for her father in the evening when he would come home wiped out after a day of legal brilliance. She understood that she was less temperamental than the rest of the family. Therefore she could be counted on. It was Polly who willingly did the chores, gave up her concert tickets when friends of the family came in from out of town, who took little cousins to the park, who knew the food phobias, likes, and dislikes of every member of her family, as well as all their clothes sizes. She knew exactly how Henry Demarest wanted the dining room table to look, his shirts to feel, his children to behave. She had been made for accommodation, and she often thought that she was spread as thin as butter on a Danish sandwich.

But Lincoln understood her. He knew when it was right not to talk to her—to give her a big, strong cup of coffee, set her in his comfortable chair, stick the hassock under her feet, wrap her up in an afghan, and leave her alone. There Polly would recline, reading whatever novel she was reading while Lincoln worked. Often she fell asleep and Lincoln sketched her.

Seeing him, Polly realized, felt the same as coming home might feel to a sailor after a long voyage. She did not mean to feel this way but it was undeniable to her that she did. Once

she had divided the world into the sort of women who had
love affairs and the sort of women who did not. But now she,
a woman who did not, did, and with considerable expertise. In
her gravest moments she gritted her teeth and said: "I deserve
this."

"Hi, Linky," she said as he opened the door.

He took her into his arms and kissed her all over her cold
cheeks.

"I am a woolly beast," Polly said.

"You are the most gorgeous, swell person that ever lived,"
Lincoln said. "Get your coat off. Where's my smoked salmon?"

Polly took a paper bag from her pocketbook.

"That's not Solo-Miller salmon," Lincoln said. "It's from
that delicatessen, isn't it?"

"Oh, Linky, I tried," said Polly. "Next time, I'm just going
to make up a huge sandwich and when they ask what I'm
doing I'll tell them: at these seminars I perform the miracle of
the loaves and the fishes. This one sandwich is going to feed
seventy-five reading technicians."

"They'll never ask," Lincoln said.

"Probably they won't," said Polly. "That's the bliss of it. I
never even have to lie. No one ever asks me what I do."

"Well, come over here, Dora, and put your arms around
me and tell me everything you've felt or thought since Friday." He held her close.

"I really do love you to pieces," he said.

"I love you to pieces, too," said Polly. "Isn't it sad?"

Once she was securely in his arms and in bed under the
covers, Lincoln told Polly that a gallery in Paris had offered
him a one-man show.

"Oh, Linky! How wonderful," said Polly.

"I'd have to be there for ten days," Lincoln said. "I don't want to be away from you for that long."

"You *must* go, Linky," said Polly. "It's only ten days."

"I want you to come with me," Lincoln said.

The effect of this statement on Polly was that of a roller coaster on a stomach. Wanting rushed from her head to her toes in a gush, making her dizzy. Instantly she realized that she had never wanted anything so much in her life. Of course, it was entirely impossible.

"Come for five days. You can fiddle it. Can't you invent some seminar in Paris? Conchita can take care of the grubs."

Conchita was the Demarest housekeeper.

"You could pull it off, Doreen," Lincoln said. "Think of what a good time we'd have."

"Not this I can't pull off, Linky," Polly said. She sat up and burst into tears. In the year since their love affair had begun, Lincoln had never seen her cry. Her big, creamy shoulders heaved. The Solo-Millers were tall and broad in the shoulders. Polly had long flanks, big shoulders, and a wide face. Her flesh was peachy and smooth. She had fine, strong hands and clear, green-flecked eyes. Polly was myopic, but her father did not believe in giving in to glasses. Polly kept her spectacles hidden away in her handbag and had spent her life squinting. Lincoln loved the smile of comfort and recognition that flooded her face once she got close enough to see what she was looking at, and she had made his heart stop one afternoon by putting on her glasses before getting into bed with him. This made him know how much she loved him.

Sundays made her more tired than she knew. Henry Demarest liked to stay in bed on Sunday morning and read the paper. Polly was up earlier than anyone. She gave the children their breakfast and took the Sunday paper and a cup of coffee to Henry. At her parents, she spent half an hour with her father who unburdened himself on one topic or another and then sat in the kitchen with Wendy who did not want any help on Sundays but had to be talked to. Then it was time to take the children to the park, or to bring them home and clean them up for lunch. Polly had fifteen minutes to herself in the study—to finish a cup of coffee, race through the paper, and be by herself. Now she was in bed with Lincoln Bennett, crying as if her heart would break.

"I can't, I can't, I can't," she wept. Then she collected herself a little. "I just can't. Oh, Lincoln, I could just manage to get away with you for those three days in Vermont but I worried the whole time that my parents would need to get me, or we would run into someone one of us knew, or Henry would call."

"Henry was in Brussels," Lincoln said.

"That made it easier. But I really was so scared. What if something had happened to Pete and Dee-Dee? Oh, it was awful."

"Awful?" said Lincoln. He put his arms around her. His darling, tactful Polly almost never slipped. It was very clear how miserable she was.

"No, it was heavenly, but it was difficult. No, I can't do it. Leaving the country is just a little too drastic."

"Then I won't go," said Lincoln. "They don't have to have me there."

"Linky, you must go," said Polly. "You have to supervise the hanging and arrangement and everything. Oh, please, please go. I'll feel so awful if you don't."

"I don't really want to, much," said Lincoln. "I'll miss you terribly, Doe. I like my molelike life with you. I always hope that when the grubs go off to college you and I can astound everyone by running off together to India on a sketching trip.

I want to always be with you like this, and when we're in our middle fifties, we'll run away."

He kissed her on the cheek. She turned to him. Her eyes were blazing. "Oh, Lincoln," she said. "I love you so very much."

At five she called home to tell Henry that she was on her way. Lincoln watched her as she got dressed. He loved to watch her slip those thick, expensive, sober clothes over her tousled hair. He liked watching her transform herself back into a respectable matron. That she took her glasses off to go home had a symbolism that was lost on neither of them. Lincoln made her a farewell cup of coffee, and they arranged their schedules.

"What do you have on this week?" he said.

"Partners' dinner tomorrow. Home Tuesday. Henry's in Boston Wednesday. Thursday, we have Paul, the Peckhams, and the Sterns for dinner. Friday we're going to the theatre with Mum and Daddy, Aunt Lila, Henry and Andreya. Saturday I can't remember—something noble like dinner with a judge. Sunday's brunch. What about you?"

"Nothing Monday, an opening Tuesday, you Wednesday, dinner with my father Thursday, and Friday I probably will go up to Gus and Juliet's for the weekend." Gus was Lincoln's older brother. He and his wife Juliet were both architects. They had a little daughter Daphne, a dog named Jip, and a Persian cat called Max, all of whom Lincoln said were architects, too, and they had a house in the Connecticut Berkshires.

As usual, it was hard for them to part, but their relationship had never had that quality of insecurity that love affairs so often have. Lincoln and Polly had declared themselves at once. Neither was very experienced at romance and saw no reason why to hide their love from one another. Furthermore, they were both well organized and were always where they were meant to be in order to make and receive telephone calls.

They knew that their relationship was possible because Polly was married. Lincoln felt that he had been born for later life, not for youth, boyish as he was. He needed his solitude. The chaos of love affairs, engagements, marriage, nest building, and child raising were not for him. But he had a loving, ardent heart, and although he did not want to marry, he wanted the security of love. In Polly he had gotten exactly what he wanted.

Polly could never have been married to Lincoln, that she knew. She wanted family life, although now she had learned that she wanted privacy as well: Lincoln was her privacy. Lincoln believed that Polly's own family protected her from her Solo-Miller family, but the truth was that the fact of Lincoln protected Polly, although she would never have thought of it. And Lincoln singled her out, as no one except her children had ever done, not for what she could do, but for what she was. Lincoln truly loved her for her spirit.

Sometimes at night, in her comfortable bed, under the blue and white early American quilt that Henry Demarest's sister Eva had given them for a wedding present, Polly thought about Lincoln and her heart was full of fear. He was so adorable, so talented, so attractive. He had enough money and came from a good family. Surely some day he would find some beautiful, adorable, talented, and attractive girl with enough money and a good family and he would fall in love with her and marry her. The nice, full life that Polly led had not prepared her for this sort of pain. At these moments she would turn to Henry Demarest who wore English pajamas and liked to read English mystery novels. He was so big, so good-looking, so safe. She was married to him, after all, and she loved him too. Didn't that thought ever cause Lincoln any pain? After these reflections it was not unusual for Polly to go into the bathroom, press her face into a large bath towel, and cry so that no one could hear her.

Lincoln's trip to Paris coincided with a long business trip of Henry's—Henry was gone the entire week. Polly went to work, took her children to their grandparents, gave dinner to her brother Paul, had her parents for dinner, and spent the rest of the time alone or with her children. Toward the end of the week it rained and sleeted. Pete and Dee-Dee and Polly sat in the kitchen and ate deviled chicken, corn sticks, baked squash, and pineapple rice whip. After the children were in bed, she had the house to herself.

She was not prepared for the violent onslaught of missing Lincoln. It was the most terrible thing she had ever undergone. Without him she felt alone on the planet, needed but understood by no one. Without Henry her life was not normal. Without Lincoln, her life was not natural. He made the Polly everyone doted on visible to Polly—there was no way to thank someone for such an amazing gift.

On Sunday Polly took the children to her parents' for brunch. The spring weather had turned cold and bright. Wendy had filled the house with vases of quince, forsythia, and white lilac. There was a little more silence than usual without Henry Demarest who was a true social asset. Pete and Dee-Dee had been given their lunch earlier and had been sent to the library to take naps. Polly, Henry, and Andreya were going to take them kite flying in the afternoon.

As usual, Polly sat in the library for half an hour with her father, and sat in the kitchen with Wendy who talked at her.

She attempted to talk to Andreya who said "yes," "no," and "of course" vigorously.

At lunch she worked hard to keep the conversation flowing —it was one of her skills. But when she was not called upon to talk, she settled back and thought of Lincoln. She carried on with him, when he was not with her, an unending conversation in her head. Stirred from that conversation, she looked up to see that he was not sitting at the table. For an instant she was surprised. It was so natural that he should have been. There was her family. She looked like them. They were her tribe, her clan, her flesh. Wasn't it odd that not one of them knew anything about what was closest to her heart?

After lunch, the children were bundled up, and Henry, Andreya, and Polly took them off to the park. Henry liked a plain, ordinary kite. He bought them at the toy store and made them more aerodynamic at home. Andreya flew a box kite. For each of the children they had a Japanese kite—one in the shape of a dragon for Pete and a fish for Dee-Dee. Polly stood on a little rise and watched. In her handbag she had the love letter Lincoln had written her from Paris. In three days he would be home. Henry Demarest was due home that evening. He had called every night, as he always did when he was away.

The wind took the kites right up. Henry's, being more aerodynamic, went much, much higher than the others. Andreya's bobbled nicely and then floated in the sky. Polly thought of Lincoln's kite which hung on the wall of his studio. It was black and silver, in the shape of a stingray, with a black and silver tail. She could never give Lincoln up, she knew. His ten days away had taught her that her love for him had become another fact in her life, like the fact of her husband and children.

The children's kites zigzagged into the sky. The dragon's

tail rattled in the wind and the fish wriggled. At the sight of those jaunty, ornamental kites Polly felt blinded by tears—of love, of missing Lincoln, of expectation. The dragon had been made so it would swoop, and when it did, Polly felt her heart break open, to love and pain. No kite, of course, had been given to her to fly, but she felt as overexcited and grateful as if it had.